Acknowlec

This book is purely ficti [illegible] my
imagination. Any character is not intended
to resemble an actual person or persons.
I appreciate all the encouragement my
family and friends have given me, especially
my husband and sister Peggy.
Please enjoy

ONE

"Jimmy… Jimmy, are you there?" Micky felt his heart would jump out of his chest.

"Christ! Micky, this had better be good. Do you realise what time it is?" he rubbed his eyes and pulled himself up in the bed. He glanced at the bedside alarm clock.

"Fuck" Micky, it's one o'clock in the fucking morning." His wife stirred "What is it, Jimmy?"

"Go back to sleep Judy, it's work."

She knew not to argue with him, so turned over and closed her eyes.

"Jimmy, I have a beauty for you. I know you'll love it." He spoke with excited babble.

An extremely disgruntled reply came back. "Couldn't this have waited till morning?"

"Sorry Jimmy, but I need to move fast, and I can get a lift down to you within the next hour."

"Okay… it better be worth it. I will meet you tomorrow at the same spot as before around midday."

With that he put the phone down and lay down to try and get back to sleep. He led there a while. His mind went over and over, it must be a good one for Micky to call him so early. This roused him and he turned over to face Judy.

"Judy… Judy, are you asleep?" he whispered in her ear.

"Not anymore." As she rolled over to face him. He took her in his arms and slowly he started to caress her. He kissed gently at first, then harder and harder until he climbed on top of her, she knew it would be quick, it always was. Before they knew it. It was over. He rolled off her and reached for his cigarettes, lit one and took a deep drag. It was always the same routine; Judy knew what would happen. A quick wham bam thank you mam and after his fag he would fall asleep. True to form within ten minutes he lay on his back snoring. She should have felt used, but although Jimmy had his faults, she cared for him. He gave her a lovely home, and whatever she wanted; he would find a way to get it. So, all in all she was happy.

Later that morning around eight-thirty, Jimmy and Judy sat in their large Kitchen drinking coffee, They had just finished breakfast. She sat looking at him. He was not drop dead gorgeous, but a tall man with powerful broad shoulders that were more appealing than a good-looking face. It was a face that dominated when required. He had a quiet demeanour at times and something about him was mysterious.

But he was still approachable. What made her heart go a flutter, made her mother's alarm go off. All his movements were purposeful and balanced, like those of a self-controlled wild animal. He would wrap himself around her until he was the only thing she thought of, and she would do anything to please him.

If she tried to think for herself… then those beautiful words that made her shiver in anticipation would disappear and be sharp.

"What are you doing today?"

"I have some business to attend to later, it shouldn't take long,"

"Ok… can I take the car? I want to visit Elaine at eleven."

"Yeah… you take the BMW I need the Range Rover."

Judy knew not to ask what for. So, she just nodded and stood up and gathered the cups to place them in the dishwasher.

He pushed his chair back and grabbed his car keys.

"I will be back later. I may have a surprise for you if you're good." He grinned and pecked her on the cheek and left the house.

Judy stood by the breakfast bar looking out the window and watched his car pull out of the drive. She could see her reflection through the glass, a well-toned body that she worked for. Obviously, she spent time on her appearance and would have her nails done, wear make-up every day. She kept her hair immaculate going to the salon once a week and wore smart clothes and heels. Fortunately, Jimmy brought plenty of money in to give her a good life.

Jimmy and Judy Morgan lived in a substantial house on the outskirts of Newquay. The properties were all impressive along the street. The grounds where well maintained by a paid gardener, and they had two garages plus a workshop.

They had four large bedrooms, all with on suite bathrooms and two good sized lounges. Although they did not need the room as they had no children. Jimmy was adamant that having a child would not be in his agenda. Judy secretly would love to have a child, but now as time went by, she had left it too long.

She took hold of her phone and called Elaine. They arranged to meet at the bistro in town.

Meanwhile Jimmy left the village and got on his phone. It rang twice and then a young woman answered.

"Hello Jimmy, are you coming over?"

"Sure thing, babe. I will be with you in five minutes. So, get yourself ready." He laughed and hung up.

Jimmy knew he had about an hour before the meeting with Micky. He thought seeing Sandy would please him no end, but he had to take care as she lived quite close. Discretion had to be met. It could be difficult at times, as Sandy was keen to show Jimmy what she thought of him. She was almost the opposite to Judy. Where Judy was tall and well-toned, Sandy was petite and busty. Judy was a strong confident woman, but Sandy was easily led and could be extremely submissive.

He pulled into a small cul-de-sac in Quintrell Downs and parked. He barely had time to lock up when he heard Sandy.

"Come on Jimmy." She cooed and gestured with a finger to come in. He turned his head from side to side quickly to see if anyone noticed his arrival. Apart from an elderly man walking down the street with his dog, no one. He sprinted across the road and quickly entered her door and closed it behind them.

Jimmy had been seeing Sandy for quite some time. She knew he was married, but it didn't stop her. He was like a strong magnet to her. Once connected, she could not resist or want to. He had that effect on women. As the door closed, he pulled her into his arms and kissed her hard and frantically as if they were teenagers again. They could not meet too often, but when they did, both were determined not to waste any time. Sandy wore a strappy dress and not a lot more apart from small delicate panties. She knew he liked it when he could get to her naked body quickly. As he pulled her straps over her shoulders she feverously pulled at his trouser button. Her dress dropped to the floor leaving her stood only in her tiny panties. He stepped back and grinned, then took a swift step forwards and swooped her up into his arms and headed for her bedroom. He threw her on the bed and rapidly pulled his trousers off and jumped on the bed. She giggled as he sat astride her and moved slowly up her body kissing her as he went. With Sandy, he took his time and care to please her.

When he reached her panties, he caught hold of them in his teeth and pulled them gently down. Moving back up her body he kissed her again up to her thighs and then kissed and caressed her deep. She wriggled and placed her hands on his head pushing him deeper and deeper. He wanted to savour every moment he had with her and then when he was ready, he thrusted into her hard and slow at first getting quicker as she cried out in ecstasy.

Just after twelve Jimmy pulled into the carpark at Trebarwith. A small rocky isolated inlet and beach, along the coast of Trebarwith Strand with a walk up a side path to get to Backways Cove. It was a good twenty-minute walk, chosen for its seclusion.

He parked up next to an old Ford Focus with two men sitting in the front seats. One of whom was Micky. sitting in the passenger seat. He wriggled as he saw Jimmy pull up and get out of his car. Jimmy left for the viewing point. He waited calmly for Micky to join him. All the time he scanned the area and fortunately hardly any others were there. He stood thinking about the time when he had checked the place out for the first time. He heard stories. It was said to be haunted, but by whom? No one really knew. The ghosts could be shipwrecked sailors drowned when their vessels hit the treacherous rocks and were torn apart. Or it could have been the restless spirit of a local man, doomed to haunt the scene of his crime. Jimmy preferred the later. Curious to know more about the crime, he had talked to a rambler on one of his visits previous. A curious twist in the tale. Many years ago, a man with two sons farmed in the vicinity, and on his death left his entire estate to his eldest son, leaving the younger one without a penny. The younger son went away wracked with jealousy. It fomented over time and turned to an obsession, until, convinced that he had been cheated of his birth right, he set out to wreak revenge on his elder brother. One night he crept onto the farm and set fire to the buildings. The blaze took hold, and the entire property was burnt to the ground. Only in the morning did he discover that his brother had died the day before and left the entire estate to him.

His thoughts were broken as Micky almost ran to him with excitement.

“Calm down Micky… flaming heck, you will attract attention. “He hissed.

“Sorry Jimmy, I just know you’re going to love this one.” He fumbled in his pocket, like a naughty schoolboy about to show rude playing cards to his friend. With his hands shaking, he pulled out a small cloth bag. Very slowly he gently tipped out the contents into Jimmy’s palm.

“Oh my god… you have done well this time Micky. Is it what I think it is?”

“Yep… A Blue Diamond. Isn’t it beautiful?”

“That’s an understatement.” He studied it close. “Where did you get it from?”

“There’s a wealthy old lady from London that might miss it.” He grinned with pride. Micky was a small-time burglar. He did not do badly for his efforts. A small stature of a man. It had its benefits. Getting into small areas and if spotted… He was often mistaken for a boy. So, the advantage had to be his size.

After a good half an hour of discussions, they agreed a price. Micky felt he should have got more but knew it would not do any good to argue with Jimmy. He had a reputation of getting his own way, nasty ways, and Micky did not want to experience this first-hand. So, jimmy took the diamond and left.

He returned home around two o'clock. Judy walked in about an hour later. She entered the main lounge and saw Jimmy sitting with a large brandy in one hand and something in the other. She could not see what.

"You're starting early today, is it a good brandy? Or bad?"

"Good..." he grinned, and he held the small cloth bag and dangled it in front of her.

"What have you got there?" she came closer to her husband and sat down next to him. He enjoyed teasing her and playfully held it up, "Hold your hands out and close your eyes."

She did as he asked, "What is it darling?"

One eye opened briefly.

"Eyes closed or you don't get it."

"Okay, okay." She wriggled on her seat excited. Gently he tipped the diamond out into her hands. The second it touched her skin she opened her eyes and squealed. "Does this mean you like it?"

"Like it… I love it. I've never seen such a large sapphire before."

"And you still haven't… it's not a sapphire. It's a diamond."

"**What**!"

"Yeah… a blue diamond. Isn't it a beauty?"

"Can we keep it?" she pleaded.

"Yes love, we have to work fast. It has to be changed though."

"What do you mean, changed?"

"Do you want a brooch or pendant?"

"Ooh… um decisions, decisions." She could not wipe the smile off her face.

"Well?" he asked.

"Brooch… yes brooch."

"Okay. Remember it will be a piece of jewellery you cannot wear for at least six months, and you tell no-one. Not even Elaine." He looked at her seriously and waited for a response.

"Yes, darling of course, you know I won't tell anyone."

"Right, first thing tomorrow, take it to a jeweller and get it done quickly." She nodded and continued staring at it.

The following morning Judy placed the stone deep down in the bottom of her bag. Before she left, she gave Jimmy a passionate kiss. "Thank you darling."

"Drive safe and keep to the speed limits. We do not want any unwanted attention. When you park up, wait for my text before you go in. Oh, and call me when you leave the jewellers."

"Will do." She left full of excitement.

Jimmy sat in front of the tv listening to the news. He wanted to know if the theft had been reported yet. Nothing…

Judy entered a small carpark in the centre of Fowey. They always went to different towns when dealing with jewellery changes to keep it away from their home. Her phone pinged and a text came through. She picked up her phone and read the message.

"Great…" she said to herself. The message read, no news… okay to go. She locked her car and holding her bag close to her body she entered the town; Judy knew Fowey quite well and went down a side street where a few little shops were tucked away.

One of which, was a jeweller they had used before.

“Hello, Mrs. Smith how nice to see you, it’s been a while.” The little man behind the counter stood with his hands resting on a glass top.

“Good morning Mr. King.” Judy always used the surname Smith and kept her conversation short and to the point, she knew it had to be this way.

“How can I help you today?” he looked at her over his small narrow rimmed glasses.

King presented himself well for a man in his later years. He barely stood five feet tall and had a little more around the midriff than he wanted. His salt and pepper hair neatly trimmed. And his clothes well-tailored.

“I have a special job for you. It needs to be completed quickly, can you, do it?”

He nodded and walked out from the counter and went to the shop door and locked it.

“We don’t want any interruptions do we.”

“True…“ She waited for his return to the counter. Judy went to her handbag. As she pulled out the small cloth bag, she stated her requirements.

"Mr. King, we can rely on your discretion?"

"Yes, yes of course you can." He watched impatiently as she held the bag.

"Okay... I want this stone set into a brooch. Can you show me some settings?"

She took it out of the small cloth bag and handed it to him. His eyes nearly popped out of his head. But he was quick to rein in his emotions and cleared his throat.

"I see... it is very beautiful Mrs. Smith, and large." He turned away and pulled out a slim drawer from behind and brought the whole drawer out and placed it on the counter. There were several settings that could be used for the stone to which Judy scanned. She found one that took her fancy.

"This one... How quickly can you do it?"

"Umm it should be a couple of weeks."

"No... that's not good enough. A week?" she looked at him firmly.

"I... I need time to set it in beautifully. I have to give it respect." He could not take his eyes off the diamond. Judy knew Jimmy would not be happy. So, she suggested

"Okay we can compromise... ten days and no longer. I want a good job or Mr. Smith won't be happy."

"Yes, yes naturally." He nodded vigorously; he could not wait to get his hands on this stone. Reluctantly she passed it over to him.

"I will be back in ten days." With that he unlocked the door and she left.

Later that night back in Newquay, Jimmy and Judy sat watching the news. A small note near the end of the main news.

"A woman in a London bureau Bishopsgate, is putting forward a reward for any information that can bring the return of a jewel taken from her home in the early hours of Tuesday morning. Anyone with information can call Bishopsgate police station anonymously if wanted".

Jimmy shot a glance at Judy; she was sat with a magazine thumbing through. So, she had not taken a lot of interest in the news.

TWO

Two years later...

Monday morning 7th June,

One hundred and fifty miles from Jimmy in Newquay. Andy stood outside in the high street in Dorchester. Both sides were rows of elegant Georgian terraced properties. He looked up at one, with its large front entrance door, painted blue. Above the door a white coated architectural fan with a small canopy. This impressive building with its windows all precisely lined up, housed a large business, Willis & Banks.

Andy took a deep breath and muttered, "Here goes." He rang the bell and seconds later a voice came from the little box fixed to the wall next to the door.

"Hello... can I help you?" The voice of a female, friendly but to the point.

"Yes... I have a meeting with Mr George Willis."

"Can you tell me your name sir?"

“Andrew Randle.”

“Come in Mr Randle and take a seat. Mr Willis will be with you shortly.”

He caught hold of the large, rounded doorknob and opened the heavy door. Entered a hallway, where he found several seats. Andy sat perched on the edge of a chair. He sat as he felt.... On edge. Why would he get a request to go to this Solicitors that he had never heard of before!!

It seemed strange to hear from Willis & Banks Solicitors. He had not applied for a job with them. That would have been a laugh. He was a more hands-on guy than a brainy head. So why contact him!

At the age of thirty-five, Andy prided himself in keeping fit. He stood a clear-cut man, with precise features, a mass of incredibly soft dark hair, and thoughtful dark brown eyes. He had a look of caution, which did change when he felt relaxed or happy, now this was not often... with these difficult days ahead.

He had always been a conscientious worker and had had several varied jobs. Always very punctual and hard working. He worked as a delivery driver and machine

He took a sip of his coffee and continued to explain.

“Andrew… I have been looking for you, for quite some time.” Andy looked puzzled.

“Did you bring the proof of identity paperwork I asked for in the letter?”

“Yes…” He fumbled in his pockets and pulled out several envelopes. He passed them to the solicitor.

“I realise that this is a surprise to you. that is why I wanted to meet you face to face.” He stopped for a moment, to look at the paperwork, then continued.

“You see, we had a client that requested an exceptional young man to take on his legacy.”

“And what makes you think I am that person?” Andy looked intrigued.

“Well… I pride myself in checking things out before I make a move. I have spent several months acquiring details of my client’s family.”

Andy sat silently dumbstruck, He thought they have the wrong person.

“Um… Mr. Willis… What is your clients name?”

“Was… He has sadly passed on. James Keely.”

“I think you have the wrong man. I do not know anyone with the surname of Keely. My name is Randle.” He would have got up to leave if he hadn’t a cup of coffee in his hand.

“Let me show you.” Willis pulled out a sheet of paper from a file and laid it out on the desk in front of Andy. On the paper he could see a detailed family tree. Willis leant forward and pointed to the tree.

“As you can see, you and your sister are there and parents. Your dad is John Randle?”

“Yes.”

If you follow up the tree on your dad’s side, you will see. His dad is Albert Randle, and Albert Randle’s dad is John Randle. Your Great Grandad.”

“Yes, I see.”

Well… your Great Grandad was married to a Matilda Keely.”

“Oh, I didn’t know that.” Andy started to gain interest.

Back in Newquay, Judy packed her bags, she started to get angrier with every item she threw in her bag. Jimmy stood watching with his arms folded. He had no emotion either way. Things had got worse as time went on and eventually enough was enough. The papers were served for the divorce and now it was time to go. Judy was not happy. She thought she should have the house, but Jimmy said he wanted it. And what Jimmy wanted he always got. There was no use in arguing with him.

"**I can't believe you are going to have that trollop living here**." She shouted.

"Stop it, Judy. She is not a trollop. She is going to be my new wife."

"**What**!" Judy spun round in horror.

"Yes… as soon as we can, we are going to marry." Jimmy grinned; he knew it would wind her up.

"You sadistic bastard." She felt cut to the bone by his look.

"Now, now Judy let us not get into another slanging match. You are doing alright out of this."

"Oh yeah, moving me into the flat. It's nothing like our home."

"Look there's nothing wrong with it. It is quite large and has beautiful views of the sea. Still if you hadn't decided to do that stupid pretty boy..."

"**What**!... What a bloody cheek. You and that..."

"**JUDY**! Don't even say it or you know what will happen." He looked menacing at her.

She stopped immediately as she knew what he meant. Instead, hurried up with the packing. She wanted to get out as quickly as possible. Clicking the cases shut, she pulled them off the bed and headed for the bedroom door.

"Wait..." Jimmy stepped in her path and glared at her.

"What now?" she attempted to stand up to him, but deep inside he frightened her. He did not mind using his fist and recently over the last two years he had tried to control her more and more, but she was having none of it. Unfortunately, there were times he won when he used his fists.

"Hand it over." He put his hand out waiting.

"What?"

"You know what, the brooch." He wriggled his fingers impatiently.

"What?"

"The Property." A large giddy smile spread over her face.

"I am not sure about it, somewhere near Druce."

"Blimey… what are you going to do?

Andy hesitated a moment then spoke softly,

"Well… this is where you come into the picture."

"What?" she looked at him not understanding what he meant.

"Becky… I told George Willis the solicitor that I wanted you to come with me."

"What!"

"I want you to come with me to see it." He looked deep into her bright blue eyes hoping she would say yes.

"When? You know I do not get much time off in the week. Only Wednesday afternoons and early finish every other Monday."

"I know… that's why I arranged for Wednesday afternoon at three. You will come with me! Please Becky, I value your opinion." He put on his puppy dog expression and kept eye contact with her. It worked a treat.

"You know I will." She smiled and leant forwards to kiss him.

THREE

Two days later, Wednesday 9th June,

Andy got up early and dressed smartly. He knew he needed to make the right impression. He had arranged to pick Becky up after work at one. This gave them just enough time to call into The Horse with the Red Umbrella, a little tearoom in Dorchester for a small bite to eat and a comfort break, before meeting George Willis.

They left Dorchester and turned left following the sign for Piddlehinton. Just over three miles they turned right onto a B road signposted Puddletown. They planned to meet in a lay by alongside the road near Druce.

As Andy pulled into the lay by, he saw a beautiful dark blue Jaguar parked up near a gateway.

"Cor look at that..." Andy loved cars and he preferred the bigger older ones.

As he manoeuvred into a better parking space, he spoke with admiration.

"It has a luxury 4-cylinder turbo under that bonnet." Becky grinned at him... she often heard him comment on cars.

He stopped and got out of his car. The driver's door of the Jag stepped out. It turned out to be George Willis. Andy turned towards the Jag and walked over.

They met halfway.

"Andrew, Hello again. You found me with no problem." It was a rhetorical question.

"Yes... I put the information in the sat nav. I hope I'm not late."

"No, not at all. I see your young lady is here." He nodded towards Andy's car.

"Yes."

"Do you want to follow me?"

"Ok... no problem." Andy turned back to his car and got back behind the wheel. The

Jag's two litre engine roared into life, and it pulled out of the lay by, gently returning to the narrow road. He turned right. About a mile up on the left the jag slowed up to a stop. He had stopped just before a large field gate.

"What's he up to?" Andy pulled up behind and sat waiting for the Jag to pull away again. Instead, Wallis got out and locked his car and waited for Andy and Becky to join him. As Becky closed her passenger door she muttered,

"Why have we stopped here?"

"Don't know… there's nothing here!" Andy looked baffled.

Willis broke their muttering as he walked towards the couple,

"I hope your footwear is suitable." He glanced at Becky in particular. Automatically she looked at her shoes and replied,

I think they're fine! As long as there are no deep puddles."

"We should be alright… there wasn't rain last night." He turned back to his car and walked pass to the front. Went and opened the large gate and entered an overgrown track that looked like part of a field.

“Can you close it behind yourselves please?”

“Sure.” Andy took hold of the gate after walking through and closed it behind Becky. They followed Willis down a track that ran alongside a low hedge on the left. On the right tall bushes invaded almost half the track hiding the view out front. Becky stretched her neck to look out ahead as far as she could.

“Uh... Mr. Willis... is there a property at the end of this track? Cos I can’t see it.”

He stopped and turned smiling at the couple, “Yes dear, there is. You can’t see it now”.

The track was uneven and because of the overgrown areas, there were times you could almost turn an ankle if you were not careful. Andy could see why Willis would not want to take his car down this lane. They walked on under a canopy of trees and out into a clearing. Where they caught sight of some outbuildings.

Upfront, Willis stopped and turned back to the couple.

“This is the property.”

“You did say it was secluded.” Andy stated the obvious.

“Yes, it is well hidden from the road.”

The outbuildings consisted of a large barn to their left and a small brick built shed.

“With a bit of work on the track, we’ve just walked down, you can drive your car and park here.”

“True.” Andy nodded, He needed to see an awful lot more to be impressed.

Directly Infront stood the large barn that had seen better days. The exterior consisted of large vertical worn boards of black and grey, faded by neglect and weather conditions. The apex roof rose high in the sky towering with a protruding hayloft.

They walked on pass the barn. Becky took a long breath and a smile appeared on her face as she turned and looked out across the fields spanning out at the front of the house and hugging the back a small, wooded area.

“What a beautiful view from here.” She did not aim her statement at anyone. She just stood in awe. It was not the property that impressed her but the trees with bluebells that lay like a large carpet on the ground.

The house itself looked ordinary at first glance. It's setting gave an impression of being hugged. The banks of trees around three sides of the house. They stood with the bluebell carpet behind, the wind felt warm on their backs as the sun shone through the trees. Willis stood with his palms raised to the sky and announced,

"Welcome to 'Meadow View'".

They stood gazing out into the woods. The atmosphere remained peaceful. All they could hear were birds singing in the trees. The views between the front and back of the house were like chalk and cheese. At the back, shade from the trees and to the front, light and bright due to the openness of fields stretching out with uninterrupted far-reaching views.

Willis turned towards the house.

"Right... are you ready to take a look inside?"

The house had seen better days, obvious neglect had not helped. Although wear and tear signs were clear, it did look quite a substantial house. With its double apex front and tall chimneys, it had once revealed itself as a truly ostentatious place.

"Yes… I'm interested to see what is like." Andy grabbed hold of Becky's hand and they followed Willis to the front door. As he unlocked the door, Andy asked,

"I can't work out why you haven't looked in the house yourself. You said you had only seen the outside."

"True… there's a good reason for that. Mr. Keely insisted no-one enter this house without the heir. That being you. He had written it in as one of his many clauses."

"One!"

"Yes… but I will go through everything when you come back to the office."

Quickly moving the conversation onto other things, he opened the door and stood back for Andy and Becky to step in.

The door opened into a long hallway with herringbone parquet flooring. The walls were covered in woodchip paper and painted a soft shade of green. The place smelt musty. A beautiful burr walnut console side table stood in the hall covered in a thick layer of dust. On closer inspection, it was a reproduction antique Queen Anne style dating from the nineteen – thirties. You could just see the quality half-moon tabletop with its gorgeous walnut grain patterns. A small tray sat on the top with some keys and a few coins. The door to their left was ajar, so Andy decided to enter this room first. It was not a big room, almost like a snug. He noticed an old piano with the lid up and its keys exposed. A sheet of music sat on the music stand. To the right of the piano stood a burr walnut bowfront chest of drawers probably made around 1870. Becky stepped towards it and ran her finger across the top.

"With a good clean, this will look beautiful. Look at the veneer and the top edge of the drawers are strung with ebony."

"It is beautiful I agree. I hope you enjoy cleaning brass."

"Why?"

"Because there are six brass handles on that." He laughed and then added.

"Don't worry, I don't expect you to do all the cleaning. I will do my share."

In front of the piano a dark wooden kitchen chair with a ladder back and placed on the seat, a small cushion flattened by someone heavy sitting for long periods.

There were some old photos set on the mantlepiece of the fireplace. Above the tiled hearth a cord hung from the side walls high up with pegs attached.

The other pieces of furniture in the room were an old tatty single chair and square low coffee table by its side. The chair had wooden flat arms that were scored and marked possibly from hot cups of drink and ingrained dirt. It would take a lot of soapy water and a good sanding down to bring the arms back to life. The fabric on the chair had not faired very well either. With a greasy mark on the back of the headrest where the head had rested and a tear in the seat. Andy stood looking at it and commented,

“That chair has seen better days, but if the padding is still in good order, it could be re-upholstered and brought back to life.”

Becky frowned, “It would need a lot of work.”

“Maybe…”

Andy turned, and they all left the room and entered another one opposite. This room looked like the main living area, more inviting. On the center of a wall at the back of the room stood a beautiful fireplace, with an Inglenook limestone surround. A large square brass box stood alongside half filled with coal. Sitting either side of the fireplace protruding into the room were two double seated settees', covered in a heavy woven faded patterned material. Turning to the right, the front windows, with dusty nets and heavy velvet dark green curtains hung. Becky walked over to the window.

"These curtains could be lovely. If they survive a wash."

"Yeah, it does look like the house hasn't had anyone to care for it in a while."

Andy stopped and turned to Willis, and asked, "What happened to Mr. Keely?"

"He was staying with friends in Cornwall, when he died."

"What... he just died there?" Becky looked puzzled.

"Well, from what his friend Jake told us, he often went down to Looe in Cornwall for a month at a time to stay with them. This time, around Christmas, he had insisted he wanted to take a walk out along the cliffs. Jake encouraged him to take their dog Blackie with him. So, he went out. It was a cold night, but James had assured his friend he would only be a short while. Well about an hour went by and Jake started to worry. So, he told his wife to put the kettle on and he would go and get James to return. He knew the route James would take. As he neared the cliff edge, he heard Blackie barking. When he reached James and his dog, he found his friend lying on the ground. He had had a heart attack and unfortunately died later in the hospital."

"Oh... that's sad." Becky turned to Andy.

"True... but at least he wasn't alone."

They continued to explore the house and naturally every room needed a good clean. Some rooms looked in better repair than others. It did not take much to see which rooms James had used more. It seemed that the main sitting room with the two settees was one and naturally the kitchen and downstairs toilet. So, downstairs there were two rooms not in use, the small first room with the piano and another room adjacent to the kitchen. The kitchen felt cramped. Becky stood scanning the room, then commented, "You know if you took out this wall between the two rooms, it could make a good-sized kitchen."

Andy smiled and said,

"Looks like you're moving in already."

Becky blushed

"Sorry... it was just a suggestion."

"Don't be silly Becky. I wanted you to come with me. You have a good eye on things."

Willis agreed,

"This house needs a woman's touch. He lived alone as far as we know."

Becky felt a little awkward, keen to change the subject,

"Come on, let's have a look at the bedrooms." She left the kitchen and headed for the stairs. Upstairs comprised of three bedrooms and a large bathroom. The room at the front on the right turned out to be the largest. It had a double bed and two double wardrobes. A bedside cabinet placed on either side of the bed. One had an old alarm clock and a dirty cup with left over tea in it. On the other side a picture frame, with an old photo of a young woman. Becky could not resist picking it up. It was a chunky rustic Jacobean wood picture frame.

"Look Andy... she was beautiful. I wonder who she was?"

"Don't know, but she obviously made an impression on James." Becky placed it back carefully as if to give it respect. She wandered across the room to the window and looked out.

"What a beautiful view from here. I can't see where the boundaries are."

"After we have looked around the house, I will show you the outside and we can walk in the garden. Well, that's if you call it a garden."

The second double bedroom had a few boxes and knickknacks. A single desk completely covered in papers and a rather tatty desk chair that had seen better days. A large cardboard box sat next to the desk with scraps of paper in.

In the small third room stood three large bookshelves filled with all kinds of books.

"He certainly liked reading." Andy stated.

Willis nodded

"I agree, there is quite a collection here."

"Do we know what he did? Like... his job before he retired."

"No Andrew, I'm afraid not. But if you like I can get you Jake's contact number. He may have some idea about James's life. I don't know how long they knew each other."

"That would be good. Thank you."

Becky stood looking at the books and reading their spine for the titles.

"There's a wide range of books here. It would be fascinating to sort these into fiction and non- fiction." Becky had always loved a good book to curl up with especially in the evening just before bedtime.

"Come on... let us have a look outside." Andy had broken Becky's thoughts on sorting books.

"Yeah.... Let's go, I could do with some fresh air. That's one thing this house needs... open windows to blow out the cobwebs."

She smiled and followed Andy down the stairs with Willis bringing up the rear.

As they reached the bottom of the stairs, Willis suggested they leave by the back door so they could see another view of the house. He took hold of the bunch of keys and fumbled to find the right key and unlocked the back door. They stepped out into a shaded area. The back garden... that they could see, was overgrown quite a bit. But looking carefully they could see a narrow path going off to the right that led down to a stream. On the opposite side of the river the blanket of bluebell started traveling through the trees.

“Is the stream part of the land?”

“Yes Andrew, you see those trees on the other side… well, they go back about twenty feet. There is a barbed wire fence that lets you know where the boundary is.”

“That’s good.” He pondered a moment, then added,

“So. Is that the land?”

“Oh goodness me no, there’s a lot more.” Willis turned to his left and said,

“Follow me.”

They walked along the back of the property and around to the side.

“Ready?” Willis asked.

“Yes…” they answered together looking at one another curiously.

Following Willis out into what only could be called a field. They walked, with the stream on their right. And walked. After a short while, Becky asked.

“How far is the end of the land that comes with the house.”

Willis stopped and turned,

"You see we've followed the stream on the right... well if you look carefully, you will see a fence alongside about three feet the other side. That's the boundary that links with the one in the trees."

He turned to his left and continued,

"The fence you see to our left follows along down behind the barn where we came in and if you look up ahead you will see a little hut." The couple strained to see it, due to the overgrowth. Andy caught sight of it first.

"Yeah, I see it."

"Well, that's the end."

"Blimey... that's a long garden, if you call it a garden." He stood dumfounded.

"I know, but it does get a lot thinner the closer you get. The land tapers off to a point. A long triangle."

"That's an unusual shape of land." Becky looked confused.

"I know, but when you reach the end, it strangely meets the normal squared fields. He smiled and added,

"Do you want to go any further?"

Andy looked at Becky, as to ask the question with a look. Then he knew the face she pulled meant no.

"I think I will leave that to another day."

So, they turned back to the house.

As they walked along the field back to the building Andy kept looking around the area. Obviously in front the house loomed up. To his right he could see across the fields and in front slightly to the right in the distance he could just see a few terraced houses that ran alongside the narrow road they had travelled earlier.

"I see we have a few neighbors." He pointed in the direction of the row of cottages.

"Yes… they are the farm workers cottages. You also have another neighbor the other side of the stream and behind the trees. The farmer, he lives in a large manor house a short way up the lane about half a mile from here." Willis had stopped to take in the views around. The three, stood silently just looking. Apart from the birds and the trickle of water in the stream, silence… very peaceful. A car drove along the lane in the distance, and they could hardly hear it.

The House would provide the perfect base from which to explore, or if you prefer, just to enjoy the beautiful surroundings in peace and solitude.

As they neared the house, Becky stated, "Well, he certainly wasn't a gardener. It would take a lot of patience and time to get this up together."

"True... not to mention, a lot of hard work." Andy turned and surveyed the area. A smile appeared on his face. He felt happy and excited at the prospect of this place. There would be only one thing that would stop him being happy here.

FOUR

Thursday morning 10th June

Back in the office of Willis and Banks, Becky and Andy sat in the hallway waiting for Willis to gather the appropriate paperwork together. They sat for a short time in silence. Andy had a worried look and Becky noticed. She leant forwards and placed her hands on his lap.

"Andy... what is it? You look as if you are going into the headmaster's office." She smiled at him and hoped he would return one back.

“Oh, you are funny Becky…” he stopped for a moment, then continued.

” Um… Becky… I have been meaning to ask you something, but I’m not sure of your answer.” He sat looking straight into her eyes with a longing stare.

“What! “

“I… do like the look of this house and think it could make a lovely home… but… only if you’re with me.” He continued to look at her, the puppy dog eyes out again.

“What are you asking me?”

“Will you move in with me? And if after a time you are happy putting up with me… we could make it legal.”

Becky took a deep breath, “I…”

The door opened and George Willis’s secretary had entered the hallway.

“He is ready for you now Mr Randle.” She turned back to the room. The couple stood up straight away and glanced at one another and followed her.

"Mr Willis what were the other clauses?"

"Right..." He shuffled some papers and found the one he was looking for.

"Okay we have achieved some already... Not to enter the house without you... Not to access bank account until you are signed up. Oh and of course, signing up on trust, to which you have done. There is more, James requires you to move in right away. He also asks for you to carry out some jobs that he has started, they are listed in his diary. Oh, and he has noted there may be more clauses in his diary."

"Where's his diary?" Andy interrupted.

"That's the thing, we don't know."

They finished up with the paperwork and left.

The couple stood outside in the street; the wind started to pick up. Andy placed his arm around Becky's waist and pulled her close.

"So... is the answer yes." He looked deep into her eyes.

"You know it is." She smiled and kissed him gently on the lips.

"We need to work out how we are going to do all this. There's so much to take in." Andy looked bewildered.

"I think we need a coffee." Becky stated and took his arm and they walked down the street back to The Horse with the Red Umbrella. They walked through the red door and headed for a table in a corner. A young girl came to their table and took their order of coffee and toasted teacakes. As they sat waiting for their order they glanced around the room. Adorning several walls were white shelving filled with oddities such as a collection of teapots. Amongst the collection were teapots with cows on, a house teapot, even a clown one. Too many to count.

Andy interrupted her gaze at the collection... "Becky... any chance you could get some time off from work?"

"Yeh I could... to be honest I will have to give in my notice and find something else closer to Druce, won't I!"

He smiled and squeezed her hand. The coffees and teacakes came and after the waitress had gone, Andy said,

"Becky... Willis said that James had a healthy bank account, so, whilst we are cleaning and settling into the house, we could live on some of it until we are ready to get new jobs."

"I can't Andy... it's your money not mine."

"Don't be silly. You will be earning it by helping me clean and sort all his belongings. I can't do it on my own."

She looked at him without saying a word for a moment or two, then reluctantly agreed.

"Well, I had better call work." She took out her phone and dialled. Surprisingly, they agreed to let her go immediately due to her difficulties with transport. She replaced her phone, grinning she stated.

" I'm all yours boss." She laughed.

Andy lent forward and kissed her.

"**Get a room**..." a man from across the room shouted, then chuckled at them as they blushed slightly.

Back out in the street Andy turned to Becky, holding up a bunch of keys he asked.

"Shall we?"

"Yeah... why not!"

FIVE

Saturday 12th June

Jimmy and Sandy had a small wedding service in the registry office. Just two witnesses, Jimmy's trusted right hand man Ken and Susan, Sandy's best friend.

Ken looked awkward in a suit. His dress code normally comprised of Jeans and T shirts. Ideal for showing off his large muscular arms that came in handy when Jimmy wanted to negotiate with unscrupulous individuals.

Susan had been friends with Sandy since primary school. They were inseparable and shared almost everything except where Jimmy was concerned. So, it was a bit of a shock when she heard her friend was to marry him. Still, it was her choice and Sandy knew Susan would always be behind her.

After the service Jimmy and Sandy returned to their home and he poured them a large glass of champagne.

They walked through the hallway and on to the kitchen. Andy carried a small box with a kettle and mugs and tea making goodies including biscuits.

“First things first... we'll make a cuppa and have a gander about while we open some windows.”

“Good idea.” Becky grabbed the kettle and ran some water, then filled it.

Cupping their mugs, they started to move from one room to another opening windows as they went. In the main living room, they stood scanning the room. On the arm of one of the settees laid a jacket. Andy went across and picked it up. As he did so it revealed a phone on the low side table. The phone had an answer machine with a light flashing away.

“Oh...” Andy stood looking at it.

“What?”

“There's messages on his phone.” Andy pointed to it.

“Oh, I see... well shall we listen?” Becky had walked over to him and placed a hand on his arm.

"Yeah… maybe he has a friend that is unaware of his death. We could let them know."

"True."

Andy leant forward and pressed the button.

"There are four new messages… Ping…first message… Hello Mr. Keely… It is Hayley from Home Safe… the lads have done all the outside work. So, on your return, can you call us to complete the installation…. Oh… Hope you had a good Christmas break… Ping… second message… Hello Mr. Keely… it is Hayley again from Home Safe can you call us… Ping… third message… beep... Ping… forth message… Hello James, it is Paul… just checking to see if you are coming to the next meeting. Do not forget it is at Charlie's this time… Oh he asked can you bring 'The Hunted?' if not call him. Bye… End of messages."

Becky was the first to speak,

"That company that left two messages, said they had done the work outside. I could not see anything done out there. It looked all overgrown."

"Yeah, I see what you mean! They're certainly not a gardening company." He laughed, and then suddenly looked curious. "I wonder if..." He turned and left the room.

"What?" Becky asked as she followed him out of the room and on out of the house. Andy stood looking at the walls and tilted his neck further to check higher.

"**Uh huh... that's what they were doing.**" He shouted as he pointed to a discreet little box on the corner of the eaves.

"What?" Becky repeated.

"Alarm system... They were fitting an alarm system."

"Oh, I see... so that's why they needed him to get back to them."

"Yeah... I think we ought to call them."

"Good idea. You call them, while I make another cuppa and I'll bring some bickies in to." She smiled and turned back to the house with Andy following. He went straight to the phone and replayed the messages, only this time, he made a note of any names and numbers.

He sat on the settee and picked up the phone, dialled the number and waited.

A young cheery female voice answered,

"Hello, Home Safe, Hayley speaking, can I help you?"

"Uh... yes I hope you can. I am calling on behalf of Mr. James Keely."

"Keely... um... yes Mr. Keely from Meadow View. I had almost given up on him. Is he alright?"

"I'm afraid not... he died about six months ago."

"Oh, I'm so sorry. I... I did not know, please forgive my comment earlier. I meant no disrespect.... I..."

"Don't worry. You were not to know." Andy interrupted.

"Are you a family member?" she asked cautiously.

"Yes, I am... I live at Meadow View now." Boy did that feel weird to say that sentence.

"I see... can you give me some details? Like your name Sir."

"My name is Andrew Randle."

"Oh!!" Hayley sounded unsure.

"I know... not the same surname. It's a long story, but if I give you the number of George

Willis at Willis & Banks solicitor's, they will verify my details."

"Thank you, Mr. Randle. Can we get you on the same number?"

"Yes, the same as Mr. Keely's." he was about to say goodbye, when he suddenly thought, "Um Hayley… does Mr. Keely owe you any money?... because I wouldn't want you to think his bill would be left unpaid."

"Oh no Mr. Randle, he paid upfront. We just need to finish the job for him… I mean for you now sir." Her voice faltered off.

"That's good. I will wait for your call to agree a time to complete."

"Thank you, Mr Randle, we will be in touch soon."

Becky walked into the room with a tray, with two mugs and some biscuits.

"Any luck Andy?" she asked as she placed the tray down.

"Yeah… they will call to arrange completing the job. They need to go through the checks first, as it is security."

"True… Well, while your there, you could call his friend Charlie and let him know about James."

“Oh, no, what do I say?” he really dreaded the thought of how to word it.

“Have your tea first, we can plan how to tell him.” She passed the mug over and he took a couple of biscuits.

“What was the name of the man that left the message?”

Andy checked his note paper,

“Paul, he’s the friend, I wonder if James could class Charlie as a friend also?”

“Only one way to find out.”

Andy dialled the number, and it rang and rang, no answer. So, he replaced the receiver back and decided to try later in the day.

“Come on, let’s get the bedroom clean and make up a bed.” He grabbed her hand, and they went upstairs. They both agreed to use the main front bedroom as their own. So, for the next few hours they cleaned every surface they could. They stripped the bed. Their mattress was due to arrive later in the day. Working as a team. They lifted the old mattress off the bed.

“Oh, look Andy.” Becky had stopped moving her end of the mattress. She pointed towards the bed frame. Lying there in front of them on the floor, a small book.

"Could that be what we're looking for?" Andy stepped forwards and picked it up.

"Well, is it the diary?"

"No Becky it's just a book James must have read at night before going to sleep." He passed it to her.

She turned it over to read the title, "The Wrong Man".

"We know one thing about James now." Andy stated.

"What?"

"He liked mysteries." He smiled and Becky put the book gently to one side so they could continue to manoeuvre the mattress out of the room. When she re-entered the bedroom, she picked the book up and took it to the small room where the bookshelves where and placed it on one of them. And stood looking again and smiled. She really could not wait to get in and sort the books out. It was a passion of hers.

Back to the main bedroom, Andy opened the wardrobes with piles of old man's clothes in.

“Becky, would you be a sweetie and pop to the car and bring some of the flat pack boxes in. I think we need to put these away as soon as possible.”

“Yeah… will do. While I am there, I will grab our toiletries. Can you hoover the floor again? I would like to get rid of as much dust as possible.”

She went down and out to the car and as she took out the boxes, she had a surprise. A large van coming down the small track. It was their new mattress.

Becky directed the two men, so they went up to the correct room. Andy looked surprised to see them,

“We’ve just got the old mattress off the bed.”

The youngest of the two men said,

“That’s good timing, do you want us to dispose the old one?”

“Can you?”

“Sure thing, it’ll only cost you a cuppa.” He joked.

“Billy!... you cheeky little bugger. Sorry mate.” His elder glared at the young one.

Andy laughed and spoke

"Listen... it's fine by us. No offence taken. You are more than welcome to some tea. You would be doing me a real favour taking it away."

"Are you sure?" The older one looked a bit uncomfortable. But Andy re-assured him.

The four sat to the kitchen table drinking tea. Becky offered the biscuits also, to which Billy took one gratefully.

"You've got a nice house here mate. The misses would love this all peaceful like." He held his cup up to his mouth and drank, adding

"and your misses makes a good cuppa."

Becky grinned, neither stating they were not married. Andy just answered quickly,

"We think we will love it here; we've only just started to move in."

"Aye lad, I reckon you'll be happy here." He finished off his tea and stood up,

"Come on Billy... we've got a few more deliveries to do. Thanks for the tea, it's just what I needed, really good of you." With that they left.

Andy and Becky returned up to the bedroom to dress the bed and make it as comfortable as possible. After the bed was completed, they started to tackle the wardrobes. They built up the cardboard boxes and one by one, they took out an item of clothing. If it had a pocket, they checked them because they decided to donate the clothes to charity shops. It felt awkward diving into someone else's pockets. But after a few, it got easier. They had a few surprises. They found some money in some, either change of a couple of notes. Pens and combs and a little notebook. In a large winter coat tucked in the bottom of a deep pocket, Andy found the diary. He could not believe his luck. He placed it on one of the bedside cabinets and they finished off packing clothes in the boxes.

Becky went into the bathroom to wash her hands, whilst Andy taped up the boxes. When she re-entered the room, Andy passed her the diary.

"Becky, can you take it downstairs with you? I am going to wash my hands and then I will join you. We can look together." He pecked her on the cheek and headed for the bathroom. Before going downstairs, she gathered up all the money and other bits and bobs and took them to.

She sat at the kitchen table waiting for Andy. As he entered, he looked surprised at the amount of money they had found. Pulling up a chair he sat next to her.

“How much did we find.”

“Twenty- eight pounds and fifty – three pence.”

“Not bad… it all adds up.”

“A bit like my tips I use to have.” She laughed.

Andy reached for the diary

“This is what I wanted to find… Now let us see what jobs need finishing.”

“I bet there’s a lot.”

SIX

Monday 14th June

On Monday morning, Jimmy left the house with a broad smile on his face. Life was good. His new wife could not do enough to make him happier. She had asked him to take the brooch to a jeweller and choose the design for her new pendant. He had asked her if she wanted to choose the design, but she said it would be more special if he chose it. So, he left to sort it out. He wanted to get it done as soon as possible. Once done, it would be the last thing that reminded him of Judy.

Jimmy parked up in St Austell and locked up. He like Judy went to a small jeweller that he had used before. The doorbell rang as he entered, and a tall thin man came from the back of the shop.

"Hello Jimmy, how's it going?" he stretched out and shook his hand.

"Good to see you, Charles. Things are good. Just got married again."

"Oh, I didn't know." He knew not to comment.

"Yeah… this is why I'm here." He took the box out of his pocket. They both went to the counter and Jimmy placed it down. As Charles opened the box Jimmy said,

"I need that brooch altered into a pendant. The new misses is not keen on it because Judy had it designed. She said it reminded her of Judy. I can see what she means."

Charles was silent and just stared at the brooch.

Jimmy had seen this reaction many times,

"I know it's beautiful. You don't see a blue diamond every day." He grinned.

"Um... Jimmy... I don't like to tell you... this is not real. It's fake."

Jimmy sat in his car with the box in his hands. He was in shock.

"The bitch, wait till I get my hands on her." He shouted and banged the steering wheel. The phone rang and Jimmy saw Sandy's name flash up.

"Christ what do I say to her?"

He answered it,

"Hi Babe's, is everything ok?" He tried to sound calm and think quickly.

"Yes love. Have you chosen my pendant design?" she sounded so excited; he could not burst her bubble.

"Not yet, I did not like the ones they showed me, so, I am about to go to another jeweller. I want it to be perfect for my perfect girl." He did his best to sound happy. She giggled and told him she loved him, and they finished their call.

He put the phone back in his pocket and started the car. As he drove, he steadily became angrier with every mile. Three quarters of an hour later he turned into a narrow lane that led to some exclusive expensive flats. As he got out of the car, he muttered to himself. “She had better be in.”

He walked up the path and reached the front entrance. As calm as he could he pressed the intercom. Judy answered.

“Hello.”

“Hi Judy love it’s me Jimmy.”

“What do you want?” she sounded cold towards him.

“I have some letters of yours.” He lied.

“You can post them in the door.

“Judy love, I wanted to see you… and… I wanted to give you something back.” He hoped this would work. She did not speak for a moment, but it did, and she buzzed him in. He did not hesitate in entering. He ran up the stairs, two at a time. She opened her door and was surprised to see him there waiting for her.

“Hello Jimmy.”

“Hi love, are you going to invite me in?”

"Well thank you for your help Jake. We will leave you to your peace. I hope the misses gets back on her feet soon." Ken got up and followed. They stepped out into the sunshine and Jimmy turned back,

"Oh, Jake what was James's surname?"

"Keely… why do you think you knew him?"

"No… I thought I might have though. Thank you." They turned back to the car and got in. Jimmy was about to start the car when a sudden thought popped into his head. As Jake stood in the doorway of his home, Jimmy dropped his window down and called. "I don't suppose you have James's address, do you?"

"Sorry no." Jake looked a bit wary, so he waved his hand goodbye and shut the front door quickly.

Jimmy looked at Ken,

"Dam…" Starting the car up they left.

As they travelled back along the route they came, Ken asked.

"So now what do we do?"

"Go on holiday to Dorset."

The phone rang in Meadow View, only twice when Andy answered.

“Hello.”

“Hello, Yes… are you, Andrew?” The male voice sounded strained.

“Yes… Do I know you?”

“Um… no… Andrew, I am Jake an old friend of James.” he hesitated a moment, then continued.

“Okay… I must tell you something James told me. It is important.”

“Right…” Andy sounded cautious.

“One night James and I were talking about his book collection and… this is where it will sound strange… He said if someone calls you asking about my books, call me right away.”

“Oh, and did you?... get a call.” Andy thought it weird he should go on about James’s books.

” No… and Yes…”

“What!”

She quickly popped her compact back in her handbag and took hold of her box and followed Jimmy around the hotel to the front of the building. The hotel was one of many terraced properties lined up along the promenade. It looked like a three-story house, but above the third floor perched above the two windows, another single window protruding out of the tiled roof. The entrance door stood to the right of a large bay window, and above this window, another of the same size.

They approached the hotel through a small metal gate attached to railings that enclosed a small front garden predominantly filled with large planters. The path they walked up, painted brick red and the doorway had a canopy above with the name of the hotel splashed across the front. At the reception, Jimmy checked in. Davey had organised a sea view room for Jimmy and Sandy. Unfortunately, Ken did not fare so well. He had a small room at the back of the hotel that overlooked the car park. They went up to their rooms to unpack and shower. The plan was to meet up later in the small bar around six-thirty for a drink before having a meal.

After their meal…around eight-thirty Davey arrived and joined them for a drink. As the conversation continued between the men, Sandy decided to excuse herself and went up to the room. Jimmy had pecked her on the cheek and whispered.

"Warm the bed up for me darling. I will be up later." Sandy could see he enjoyed time with the lads, so she told him to take his time as she would not be going anywhere.

As she left the room. Davey commented, "You've got a good un there."

"I know, and the packaging isn't bad either." Jimmy smirked.

"You lucky bastard." Davey raised his glass to Jimmy and drank back his whisky.

"Want another?" he asked.

"Yeah, why not and you can get them in."

As Davey went to the bar to get more drinks, Jimmy whispered to Ken,

"We could do with extra help, but not a word about the diamond." He stared at Ken fiercely waiting for confirmation, to which Ken nodded immediately. Davey returned with the drinks and placed them on the table. As he sat down, Jimmy spoke,

"Thanks for sorting out the rooms for us."

“That is exceedingly kind of you. Can you please inform the others what has happened?”

“Yes, I will.”

Andy put the receiver down and turned to Becky,

“He sounded a real nice bloke. The reason why James has so many books is because he is in a book club.”

“I see… that’s something I would love to do… I mean I would love to be in a book club.” She smiled.

“Well, we’ve been invited to their book club one evening, so we can find out more about James.”

“That’s good of them, I look forward to that.”

After tea, they snuggled up on the settee. The television was on quietly in the background. Becky was reading a book and Andy studied the diary.

`“Hey, it’s an eye opener to some of the thoughts of James.”

“What do you mean?” she put her book down briefly.

"Well, it looks like around easter time last year, he went down to Cornwall."

Andy turned a page and continued to read aloud.

"Lily has come up trumps again. I have a box of books to add to the collection. The lads will be happy. I leave for home in the morning. So, I will go through them when I get back."

Becky interrupted saying,

"Okay... so we know he had the books. I wonder if there was something special about Danny's book. If James found it... He may have written something about it later on in the diary."

"I will carry on reading through just in case." Andy continued to read it to himself.

NINE

Sunday 20th June

There was a chilly wind coming in from the sea at the group of police on the isolated stone beach close to Trebarwith. Detective

David Taylor from the Cornwall and Devon police headquarters in Austell stood looking at a dead body strewn out on the rocks. It was in a bad condition, due to the sea water and rocks and what looked like animal interference. It looked as though it had been there for days, if not weeks.

"Who found this woman Sergeant Wheely?"

"A Mr. Lyons Sir. He is sat in a police car up in the car park."

Taylor nodded in approvement,

"Very sensible Wheely to keep him away from the scene. I want this whole area cordoned off, including the pathway at least a hundred metres either side to start with."

"Yes sir." He turned to a PC Shears and instructed him to implement Taylors wishes.

Detective David Taylor was good at his job, but not an easy man to get on with. He liked things his way and this sometimes meant he would not listen to others' opinions. This would slow down active investigations. Although when he eventually listened, and a result was attained strangely he would take all the credit. It could be very frustrating working alongside Taylor. He was nearing retirement. Only a couple of years to go. You could say he was an arrogant man, but he could organise a team quickly and efficiently. Those that drew the short straw ending up working with him, knew to act fast when a request was made by him.

Sergeant Wheely was that officer today. He had reservations about working with Taylor. But he kept reminding himself, only a couple of years to go and then maybe he would get a chance for promotion. If he worked alongside Taylor, he might put a good word in for him. Okay maybe not.

“Where’s the forensic team?” Taylor shouted.

“I think they have just arrived sir… I will check.” Wheely moved away quickly towards the pathway. He started to climb up towards the top edge of the rocks when he caught sight of the team.

As they came close to him, he caught a mumbled question.

“So, what sort of mood is the old bugger in today?” It was the medical examiner Jerry that spoke. He was a short man of small stature. He had the attitude that they, the police officers needed him so he could say what he wished… within reason. There were times he almost got in trouble with the higher bosses when he overstepped the mark. But it did not stop him pushing his luck. He enjoyed watching the sergeants squirm uncomfortably in front of him. Wheely just made a face as to say he's in his normal mood at the start of a new case. He turned back and followed the forensic team down towards Taylor.

"Okay... we are here. So, everyone out." Jerry enjoyed this part, barking an order towards Taylor. To which he always got the same response,

"Hey Jerry remember who you're talking to." And a face like thunder, it worked every time. Jerry just grinned and set to his job. After a few minutes Taylor asked,

"So, what can you give me to start with?"

"Christ... Taylor... give me a chance." Jerry stopped what he was doing and turned to him.

"Anything would help."

"Ok... we have a female dead body."

"So, is it murder?" Taylor was always impatient.

"Cannot say yet... it could be due to a fall from the rocks. Oh, wait a minute... Definitely murder. On quick inspection, I would say it is strangulation. She has red spots in the eyes and swollen lips. I will confirm more when we get back to the lab."

Photos were taken and little bags filled with small various items from around the body. Taylor decided to leave the team to their work.

"Sergeant... you stay with the team and report back to me later."

"Yes Sir."

Taylor walked up to the car park where Mr. Lyons sat in the police car. He was getting impatient, and the poor PC left to keep him there was getting a right ear full.

"How much longer do I have to stay in this ruddy car?" he ranted.

"Not much longer Mr. Lyons." Taylor answered as he opened the back door of the car. He continued,

"We do appreciate your patients."

Mr Lyons looked a bit sheepish as he shook hands with Taylor.

"Very briefly, can you tell me how you came to find the woman down on the beach?"

"I was taking a short cut back to the farm, when I saw a flock of birds close to the about his old man getting banged up. It was not the boy he told... But a nasty piece of work, Tommy Lucas. He overheard and revelled in spreading it around the school. Then Ken constantly got called jailbird bait. He could never work out why. So, from then on, he decided he would be the one that controlled a situation and as he was a big lad, he used his size to get what he wanted. As time went by, he started to follow in his dad's footsteps. Apart from getting caught... yet... When he pulled up a chair and sat, he nodded a thanks to Jimmy,

"Morning Mrs. Morgan."

Jimmy quickly jumped in saying,

"Ken... you can call her Sandy you know."

"Oh, I don't mind... it's nice to be called Mrs. Morgan. I am still getting used to it. But yes, Ken please call me Sandy. I'd like to think friends of Jimmy are friends of mine."

"Will do Sandy." He grinned and reached for his coffee. It smelt good and the heat of the cup as he cradled it, warmed him up quickly.

"It's a bit chilly out there this morning."

"I bet it is. What made you go out?" Jimmy asked.

“I went out for a newspaper.” He glanced at Jimmy as if to say you know why. He raised his eyes at Ken as to question him. As discreetly as possible, Ken shook his head. Jimmy physically relaxed in his seat.

“So, Sandy love, what are you going to do today?”

She hesitated for a moment,

“Well, as it’s a bit cold… I think I will do a bit of shopping. Then I will have a nice long soak in the bath… You won’t be out all day, will you?”

She glanced at him playfully. A look that gave Jimmy a message of if your home early you have a treat to look forward to. It was chocolate for his ears. Jimmy stood up and leant forward to kiss her. As he did, he whispered in her ear,

“I knew why I married you…Come on Ken, we have work to do.”

Jimmy walked out of the lounge and headed for the rear of the hotel, with Ken close on his heels. They got in the Range Rover and sat for a moment.

“Jimmy… where are we meeting Davey?”

“Dorchester… Top of town car park. There’s a café in the car park.”

Davey turned left down a hill and at the bottom he followed the road round to the right. Then almost as soon as he had, he braked to turn left up to a dead end. Jimmy almost went up the back of him and swore.

At the top end of the dead-end road hidden by other small units, was Davey's small lock up. He felt a little uncomfortable about bringing them here, but he could not think of anywhere else. So, he went to a small side door and unlocked and waited for Jimmy and Ken to catch up. Both Ken and Jimmy stood briefly scanning the area. The majority of the small units were red brick single storey. Some had a roller door and a single door and a narrow window that surely was a toilet. Others had the normal door and narrow window plus another wider one. Davey's was one with a roller door in front. But unlike some of the others his small door was on the side. The place looked run down and in need of a lot of work. But it suited Davey no end as not many people came up as far as the top end of this narrow road. This meant his business dealings stayed private.

They entered directly into a small room that should be used as office space. Davey had a few boxes and in the back corner a grubby small sink with a small wall cupboard above. There were two chairs and a table sat on the left as they entered. To their right another door that led into the open area behind the shutter door.

"Will this do? I have a small radio I can put on in the background."

Jimmy stood taking in their surroundings, "Well, I suppose it will have to."

He walked to the table and threw the notebook down on the top. Then dragged a chair out and sat down.

"Come on, sit down Davey. I need you to read this to me in a voice that sounds like it is educated. Can you do that?"

Davey pulled out the second chair and sat next to Jimmy and then picked up the notebook so he could read the words to himself first. He cleared his voice and read...

"Hello Sir... I am calling from Liskeard Hospital; do you have a moment? I need to tie up a loose end. We at the hospital like to ensure personnel items from the deceased are returned to their rightful owners." He stopped a moment...

"What are you saying we have of this bloke?"

“I have not thought of that yet.” Jimmy admitted.

“Could be his watch.” Ken suggested.

“Good idea Ken mate… Right continue Davey.”

“Um… If he asks what personnel items…” Davey looked up and smiled at Jimmy.

“I can say a watch… okay?”

“Right… and this is where you get his address so you can send it to the next of kin.” Jimmy grinned.

ELEVEN

Back in Meadow View, Andy and Becky had finished their inventory and most of the cleaning. So, Becky announced she could not wait any longer. She wanted to sort out the books in the small bedroom. Andy smiled and gave her a kiss.

“Okay while you sort books, I am going to try and tidy the small area out the back. A bit of weeding.”

“So, you are not going to tackle the long garden?”

“No way.” He laughed as he headed for the back door.

Becky poured herself a glass of orange and took it up to the small room. She knew books could be dusty and she thought having a drink would be a good idea.

There were shelves reaching up to the ceiling and almost all were crammed with books. Some were sat up like soldiers and others laid down sleeping.

Becky stood looking at the task ahead and murmured,

“Now… let’s see if there is any order with these books first.” Reading the sleeves and mentally trying to see if there were any kind of pattern presenting itself. On close inspection she did notice a few books were grouped together. But… it looked like James had given up and just placed books where he could fit them.

“Well… I have my work cut out.”

She decided to pull books off the shelf and at first would place them in three piles. Fiction and nonfiction and one pile for biographies. At one point Becky wondered if it was such a good idea when she stood and stretched her back and saw the piles getting higher by the minute. But... yes it had to be done even if only to clean the wooden shelves from thick dust. With the empty shelves in front of her, she started the task of cleaning and polishing the wood. The cloths were thick with dirt, but the shelving came up a treat. The rich dark oak shone from the sunshine streaming through the window. Becky went to the bathroom and washed her hands. On return to the bedroom, she went to the window and looked out onto the back garden. Andy was knelt down by some flowers pulling at what looked like clumps of grass.

"How are you getting on?" she called from the open window.

He almost toppled over as the grass had suddenly released itself from the grip of the ground and with Becky's call. He turned his head upwards,

"It's a slow job. It will take a long time to get this lot in control. How about you Becky... Are you winning?

"Well, the bookcase is clean… but now I have to put the books back. Wish me luck." she laughed

"I will leave you to it."

"Thanks a bunch…" He replied with a grimace but quickly followed by a chuckle.

Becky disappeared back in the bedroom to continue her sorting and re-stacking the books.

Andy stayed on his knees and just gazed around the bit of garden he could see. He smiled to himself, how lucky he was to have this house and garden even if it looked a mess. It would certainly be a challenge and probably take a whole day just to sort this small piece at the back. Thinking on the length of the side part, he grinned and said to himself,

"When I can afford it, I will get a ride on mower." He always dreamed of one but had never had a garden big enough. Now he did and if it were in his power financially, he would buy one. But first he would have to buy some decent tools like a good strong fork and spade to tackle these clumps of grass.

As he continued to pull out weeds and grass his mind was working overtime. He thought on how come he never knew James Keely was even a relative. Andy thought he must try and get his dad to open up and tell him more about the family. He decided to call him later, maybe after tea. He just kept remembering his grandad's words, "leave it boy, you don't want to know." But Andy did.

Back up in the bedroom Becky had started to put books back on the shelves. She noticed there were a few books with the same author. So, she decided to put them together and in alphabetical order. Some authors she recognised whilst others were unfamiliar to her. The fiction books varied from mysteries to crime and some romantic. This surprised Becky, for some reason she could not imagine James wanting to read romance books. Still to be honest there were more crime and mystery than anything else. Whilst setting the books in alphabetically by authors surnames, she came across several with the surname of Smith. So, she decided she would have to do these by the initials or first name also. One book by L. R. Smith caught her attention. Not by the title, 'Stolen' but by the weight of the book. She took it and looked thoughtfully at it. She opened the book, why? She was not sure. But had a surprise.

In Davey's lock up, Davey had familiarised himself with the details Jimmy wanted him to ask this Solicitor.

"So, who's this solicitor I have to call?"

Jimmy took out his note,

"A George Willis of Willis & Banks in Dorchester."

"Why didn't we just call in as we were only a stone's throw away earlier."

"Davey you idiot... I do not want anyone knowing who I am. That's why I am getting you to call with this story." Jimmy looked exasperated.

"Okay Jimmy... no need to get testy." Davey raised his hands in a slightly protective manner.

Whilst Ken looked at him as if to say that was a stupid thing to say. He knew Jimmy had laid out men before for less than what Davey had said. To be honest Jimmy would have if he did not need him to do the call.

"Right clear your throat and read out a bit of the sentence to me. I want to hear your voice." Jimmy barked out the order.

Davey nodded realising he may have overstepped the mark and was lucky not to have paid the price. He coughed once and started to read. Jimmy listened and interrupted.

"What!"

"Slow it down and try and sound relaxed and friendly... you sound like you've got verbal diarrhoea."

Davey tried again and Jimmy nodded in agreement that he was happy for him to go ahead.

With the radio on in the background, Davey picked up his phone and tapped in the number.

" Hello... I am calling from Liskeard Hospital; do you have a moment?" He waited for the reply. A woman on the other end asked,

"What was the nature or the call and to whom did he want to speak to."

"Um... I am led to believe the man I need to speak to is George Willis, and I am ringing about a James Keely." Davey looked up at Jimmy hoping he was happy with the start.

"I will see if he can speak to you. Would you mind waiting?" She put the phone on hold and music played in the background.

Davey sat waiting and Jimmy looked agitated and mouthed

"What's happening?"

"I'm on hold." He whispered; Davey was about to add something when the woman on the other end came back to him.

"Hello..."

"Hello, any luck?" Davey asked.

"I am sorry, but Mr. Willis is with a client at the moment. Can you call back? Or give me your number and I will get him to call you as soon as possible."

"Um... just one moment I will ask my colleague what he wants me to do." Davey placed his hand over the phone and whispered,

"Jimmy... he's busy they want my number, or we call back. What do I do?"

"Tell them you will call back and ask when the best time is to catch him."

So, Davey related this to the woman and waited for her response.

“Alright I would say around eleven-thirty. What’s your name?”

“Oh... James Forester.” He answered quickly, then shut the phone off.

“What the hell is that about? Who’s this James Forester?” Jimmy raged.

“It was the first name I could think of. I was not going to give my own.”

Jimmy calmed down a bit and said,

”You better write it down, so you don’t forget it.”

He nodded and grabbed a pen and scribbled it down.

“Do you think she believed you?”

“I think so... I hope so.

Becky ran down the stairs two at a time and out to the back of the house to find Andy.

Full of excitement she called,

“Andy... look what I’ve found.” She passed the book to him.

"Yeah, a book... Stolen. What's so special about it?" He looked puzzled.

"Look at it closer."

He turned it over in his hand still not sure what he was looking for.

"Open it, Andy."

"What?"

"Open it."

He slowly opened the book.

"What the heck!"

He could only open up the hardback cover, as the rest of the pages were stuck together. The centre of the pages had been cut out. It would make a good hiding place for something.

"Wow... I see what you mean." He looked at Becky in bewilderment.

"What would James want to hide in a book?" Becky asked.

"Strange... another question where it is now?"

"Blimey... what was he up to... or in to?"

"God knows. I hope it was nothing bad. I don't know why but I would like to think he was a good man." Andy looked a little worried.

Becky touched his shoulder, then she gave him a hug.

"Come on, let's go inside and have a cuppa and a sandwich. You look like you need a break." She smiled and turned for the house.

"Yeah, why not...."

They sat to the kitchen table sipping tea and just looking at the open book laid on the table in silence.

Suddenly Andy pushed back his chair and went to his notebook. He found the phone number he wanted and grabbed his mug of tea.

"I'm going to call Jake; I hope he may be able to shed a light on this and give us some answers."

"Good idea. You never know he may know a good reason for this book." She stood up grabbing her mug and followed him into the living room.

They sat on a settee and Andy rang Jake. After a few rings he answered.

"Hello Jake, it's Andy, James's relative." He waited for a response.

"Oh, hello young man how are you and your young lady settling in?"

"Very well thank you. It still feels a bit strange going through his things."

"I don't think you will have much to sort through and probably no surprises." He chuckled.

Andy looked surprised.

"Well… it's funny you should say that. Um… Jake, did James have a reason to hide things?"

"What do you mean hide things… what things?"

"Well, we are trying to work that out ourselves."

Jake went silent for a moment. So, Andy continued.

"We found a book…"

"He had a lot of those Andy." Jake answered but in a joking way.

"I know… It was while Becky sorted them, she came across a special book." Andy deliberately stopped a moment to see if

Jake would jump in. But he did not, so Andy continued.

“What makes this book special… is someone has cut out the centre pages to make a hiding place for something.”

“Well, I can tell you something, it was not James. He loved his books too much to cut one up.”

“Oh… that’s weird.”

“Sure, is lad. Oh, you may get a call from either the solicitors or Liskeard Hospital. They say they have something of James that they wish to return to you. I did not want to give the young woman your number.”

“Thank you, Jake, did you get her name?”

“You know I didn’t sorry, she said she worked in the office in the hospital.” He sounded a little concerned.

”Do you think I ought to call George Willis and warn him?”

“You could… or would you like me to call him?”

“I will let you, if you don’t mind.”

“No problem. Thank you for letting me know.” They chatted for a short time and then said their goodbyes. Andy sat and relayed the conversation. She was surprised to hear that James had not cut out the book, and curious what the hospital had that belonged to James.

“I think I will call George Willis now to warn him to expect the call.”

“Okay, while you are doing that, I will make us the sandwich I promised. She stood up and bent to kiss him.

Elizabeth the secretary of George Willis answered the call quite quickly. It took Andy off guard.

“Oh um… is Mr Willis free? It’s Andy Randle.”

“I’m afraid he is with a client at the moment, can I help?”

“To be honest I just wanted to let him know that he will get a call from Liskeard Hospital. Jake had a visit, but the young woman did not give her name.”

“That’s peculiar… we have had a call about half an hour ago. But it was not a woman. It was a man, and he did not sound like he knew what to say. He had to check with his superior.”

“Did she come on the phone.”

"No... it was another man. I did not speak to him; I just heard his voice in the background, he sounded agitated. The other one asked what to do when I said Mr Willis was with a client. They said they would call back around eleven-thirty."

"Hmm... sounds strange to me."

"Maybe, but I'm sure Mr Willis will sort it out and be in touch."

"Thank you."

TWELVE

"It is eleven-thirty, are you ready?" Jimmy asked.

"Yeah, I suppose so." Davey did not sound confident and felt reluctant to go through it again, but he knew he did not have a choice. Jimmy's persuasion tactics were well known. So, he took hold of the phone and re-dialled the solicitors. The same woman answered the phone and spoke

"Mr. Willis will speak to you now."

Davey did a thumbs up sign to Jimmy. He grinned and waited.

"Hello… Mr. Forester, how can I help you?"

"Uh… oh yes… Mr. Willis… I am calling from Liskeard Hospital in the offices. We have some belongings of a Mr…" Davey pulled the pad closer and read.

"Mr. James Keely."

"Oh yes… you have had them a while. He has been gone for several months." George Willis sounded guarded.

"Yes, I am sorry about that somehow it was overlooked so, we want to tidy up loose ends and get them to his relatives." Davey physically took a breath. He had not realised he had almost stopped breathing as he spoke.

"Yes, fine, if you send it to me, I will forward it on to them."

Davey looked exasperated.

"Uh… would it not be easier if we sent it straight to them?"

"So sorry I could not give you their details without speaking to them first."

"Fine if you could call them and then we can send it direct." Davey sounded convinced he was doing well.

But George Willis decided to stand his ground,

"I will take delivery of the items and get them to my client. I will put you back to my secretary and she will give you, our address." Before Davey could protest, he had sent the call back to her.

"Hello, Mr Forester, do you have a pen?" All Davey could do was to answer yes and write down the address as she dictated it.

"Fucking hell... why did they refuse to give you the address? You can't have come across strong enough." Jimmy was fuming.

"You heard me Jimmy... I... I could not persuade him. The miserable old sod."

Ken was listening and wanted to calm things down,

"Well, Jimmy, we have to find another way." He placed his hand on Jimmy's shoulder hoping to cool him.

Back in Dorchester at the solicitors, George Willis asked Elizabeth his secretary to get the number of Liskeard Hospital for him. She did so and he picked up the phone and rang them.

“Hello, Liskeard Hospital, which department do you require?” A young woman asked.

“Can you put me through to the office that deals with personal belongings?”

“Sorry sir… is it lost property? Or returning personal belongings.”

“The later.”

"Ok sir, one moment.”

“Hello, how can I help you?” This time a man’s voice that sounded firm but friendly.

“My name is George Willis from Willis and Banks Solicitors. Do you have a James Forester working for you?”

“I am afraid I cannot divulge names of any employees.”

“Alright, then can I ask if any of your department has contacted my offices in Dorchester in the past say half an hour, regarding my client Mr. James Keely?” he waited for his response.

He could hear him tapping on a computer.

“I am sorry sir, the only contact concerning a James Keely was well over six months ago and that was to the same company, but in Devon.”

“Thank you for your time, you have been very helpful.” He replaced the phone and sat a while. Looking through his contact numbers he found Jake’s number.

“Mr Willis, Andy told you then. Have they contacted you yet? “Jake sounded quite jolly.

“Yes Jake, they did. Can you tell me exactly what this woman said and anything that has happened relating James recently?”

“Sure… is there something wrong?” Jake asked curiously.

“Well, it has to be a co-incidence that this woman and man have the same story.”

“A man!”

“Yes… but I will tell you more. First can you tell me about the woman please.”

“She just turned up on our doorstep. She said she came from the hospital.”

“Did she name the hospital?”

Jake was quite for a moment thinking,

“Do you know, I don’t think so, no.”

“Interesting… carry on.”

“Um… where was I? oh I know. I invited her in, and she seemed very pleasant. She told us she worked in the office at the hospital and that they had come across some personal items of James that they wanted to return to his relatives.”

“Did she say what these items were?”

“No… I must admit I felt a little awkward with the situation so. I did not give any details of James address or contact number.”

“Good… So, let me recap… she never told you what hospital she came from and …”

Jake cut in,

“Oh dam… I have just remembered that Mary the misses did mention the hospital by name when she spoke of how busy they are. So, she could have told her.”

“Don’t worry Jake it is easily done. Were there any other incidents concerning James?”

“Yes… two men turned up a few days ago, they gave a story about a book James had purchased from my dear friend Lily…” He went silent for a moment. Then he relayed as much as he could remember about the visit. When George heard everything, he instructed Jake to contact the police straight away.

“Why?” Jake could not see what they would be able to do as they did not know their names. And nothing was stolen.

“I am not sure if it is anything, but they are up to something.”

“Oh… my… God!” Jake felt terrible and fear flooded through his veins.

“We could be in danger!”

“Ok… keep calm Jake. What I want you to do is put the phone down and call the police right away. If they do not come out immediately, then call me back…Alright?”

“Yes… Yes, thank you Mr Willis.” He put the phone down and just sat stunned for a moment. Then he picked up the phone again.

The doorbell went.

“Mary, can you get that please.” Jake asked as he checked the number for their local police station.

THIRTEEN

Jimmy just got off the phone.

“Any luck Jimmy?” ken enquired.

He gave the thumbs up and turned to Davey.

“Right Davey… what am I going to do with you?” he gave a knowing look that Davey did not like.

“What do you mean Jimmy. I did everything you wanted. You know I won’t say anything to anyone.” He babbled in panic.

Jimmy picked up Davey’s phone and opened it.

“Who is the young lady in this picture?” He pointed to the photo on Davey’s phone.

“That’s Lisa my partner.”

“Very pretty... it would be a shame to lose such beauty.”

Davey panicked,

“Look Jimmy, you can trust me to keep my mouth shut.”

“I hope so, for Lisa’s sake.” Jimmy gave Davey a long stare. If the floor could swallow him up Davey would be incredibly happy.

“Alright, I am going to trust you... for the moment. But you know what will happen if you let me down. It will not be, only Lisa. Do I make myself clear?”

“Yes... yes.” Davey was extremely glad he had been sitting down, because if not he would have crumbled in a heap.

“Come on Ken, we need to get back to the hotel. I have a new young wife waiting for me.” He grinned and winked.

Out in the car Jimmy set the sat nav up to check how long the journey would take, so he could call Sandy and give her a rough time he would be back. He wanted to make sure she would be there waiting for him. Jimmy had a controlling streak in him. But as long as his women made him happy, they would be rewarded. He could not see a problem with that. Although it was the other reason Judy left him, but the main one was Sandy.

As they travelled, he informed Ken of the conversation he had earlier just before they left Davey.

“I had to call on Eddie and Ross.”

Ken looked confused,

“What’s going on Jimmy?”

“I have no choice. I had to call Eddie and Ross to help, as they were the nearest and I can trust them.”

“You are still not making any sense.”

“Look… I need the address and quick. The only one who has it, is this old man, Jake. We are in Dorset, and he is in Looe. So, Eddie and Ross have gone to fetch it one way or another.”

“What! Are you mad?”

Jimmy glared at Ken,

"It's a bloody good job I did not hang around in getting them in."

"What do you mean?"

"They were about to do another job. They promised to get right onto it."

"Oh, bloody hell Jimmy you are lucky there."

"Yeah. Eddie will call me later when he has what I need."

Back in Meadow View Andy was washing up and Becky wiped the dishes. They both stopped suddenly when they heard the letterbox bang. Was it post for James? Or… maybe it might be their first post. They looked at one another and grinned. Andy quickly dried his hands and went into the hall to see the post. It turned out to be a small parcel addressed to Mr. A Randle, Meadow View… He held it for a while just looking at it. He read it to himself just to double check it was for him at this address.

"I have a small parcel." He called to Becky as he walked into the kitchen.

"I wonder if it is the journal Jake was going to send you."

“Yeah, it could be.” He unwrapped it and she was correct. A small brown leather-bound journal that looked like it had seen a lot of use.

“I wonder what he wrote in it.” Becky moved closer to Andy to see.

“Let’s see shall we.”

They both went into the living room and settled on a settee together. At the start of the journal there were a lot of ramblings about everyday things. Subjects like James plans for his garden and home. On one page there were details about a burglar alarm… like contact numbers and costings.

“Well James had sorted that out.” Andy stated. He turned another page. Just a small sentence affirming the date the company were to start the first fix, just before his trip to Jake and Mary.

On the next few pages were notes on his time spent in Looe. James certainly enjoyed his time there. He wrote fondly of his friends.

After Christmas, the tone of his writing seemed to change.

December 27th ‘I have a few more days before I go home. I have hidden it so I can think what to do. Maybe I should tell Jake about it…'

The following page he noted, 'Not feeling too good today, maybe I will sit out overlooking the sea. It may help me think. I have to leave clues where to find it if something should happen to me. Should I tell Jake? No… I cannot be sure it came from Lily.'

"Blimey Andy do you think he knew he was going to die?"

"No Becky… but maybe he knew he was not right and feeling quite poorly."

They turned another page. On this one a title 'Clues'

Where did it come from…? Who do I trust?

Note… for whoever has my journal.

If you have found 'Stolen' and you are my heir. Then you have started the journey.

But if you are not…then it will be lost for ever.

Andy turned to Becky with a puzzled look. "What does he mean?"

"I haven't the foggiest!"

"Do you know what I think? We need to go to this book club."

"Why?"

"Well, remember what Charlie said… the book club could tell us more about James."

"True. We may be able to fathom out how James brain worked and with that we may be able to find whatever he hid." Becky smiled.

Andy called Charlie and he said that they were going to meet up tomorrow evening and they would be welcome to join in. He gave Andy his address and they noted down the time.

Jimmy went straight up to his room and as expected Sandy lay on the bed waiting for him. She had bought a new negligee and was keen to show him. As he had a bad day, this was just what he needed a distraction. The type he could never refuse.

After a shower and change of clothes the couple went down to the bar. Jimmy ordered a large Brandy and lemonade for Sandy and a large whisky for himself. Just as he paid for it, Ken walked in.

“Oh, barman… get another whisky for my friend please.” And he passed more cash across the bar.

“Thanks Jimmy I think I need it.”

Jimmy gave him a quick glance as to say careful what you are saying in front of Sandy. Ken acknowledged him with an apologetic nod. The men walked away from the bar and went over to a cosy corner where Sandy sat waiting for her drink.

“Good evening Sandy.” Ken nodded to her.

“Hello ken.”

“Would you mind if I join you?”

“Of course not.”

They sat and took a mouthful of their drinks. Jimmy did his best to keep his mind away from his dilemma by asking Sandy what she did today.

“I went shopping as you know.” She stopped and winked at him. Then continued.

“I found a lovely little coffee bar where they do a great cappuccino, you must come with me and try it, Jimmy.”

“Yeah, I will babes I promise soon.”

“Do you have to work tomorrow?”

“I am sure we will… but not sure what time. It depends on a phone call.”

“So, you may have more time tomorrow,” she gave him a look like saying please.

“Look love, as soon as I get the call, I can tell you then alright.” He sounded a little agitated as his mind filled again with his problem. Fortunately, he did his best to suppress it and added,

“Sorry love I didn’t mean to sound grumpy. It has been a trying day hasn’t it Ken.”

“Yeah, it has.”

“Anything I can do to help Jimmy?”

“No babes… you are doing just fine.” He leant forwards and kissed her tenderly.

“Hey, you two want to be alone. I will leave you to it.” Ken was about to leave when Sandy suddenly stopped him with her hand on his arm.

“No, don’t be silly Ken you are not going to eat alone and besides you are our friend.” She smiled and winked as she took another sip from her glass.

Jimmy’s phone rang. He stood up and said, “I won’t be a moment love… work.” As he stood up and walked out to the foyer. No one was around which gave Jimmy a good place to take the call.

Eddie was on the other end.

"Jimmy... can you talk?"

"Yeah mate, what do you have for me?"

"We did as you asked. Got there just in time to stop the old bugger from speaking to the cops."

"That was lucky."

"You're not kidding.... Mind you the misses made a lot of noise about it."

"You did have your faces covered, didn't you?"

"Yeah, we did Jimmy, what do you take us for? Idiots!"

"Sorry Eddie, no offence meant. It's just been one of those days."

"None taken... as I was saying the misses was making a row. So, Ross put a gag on her. She soon shut up then. "

"What about Jake? What did he do?"

"He kept repeating don't hurt her. I told him to keep quiet and they wouldn't get hurt."

"What did you get?"

"We took a few bits and bobs, but they didn't have a lot of quality stuff. A bit of cash that will go to paying for our trip down to Dorset."

Jimmy started to get impatient,

"Did you get what I wanted?"

"Yeah, eventually we found it in a drawer under the telephone. These people have no imagination." He laughed.

"You did take other paperwork and things?"

"Yes..." this time it was Eddie getting frustrated. Before Jimmy could ask more, he added,

"I tipped the drawer out into a bag and took the lot. He will not know we were after a certain item. Oh, and we ripped out the telephone so they could not call for help."

"Did they see your car?"

"No chance. We parked on the street a short distance away and to stop them watching us go, Ross did his speciality, tied them up. It will take them some time to get out of that."

"Good job Eddie. As you did not get much out of the job like jewellery, I will see you alright."

"Thanks' Jimmy, I will call you tomorrow morning when we are about half an hour away and we can meet you in an appropriate place."

With that he hung up. Jimmy walked into the bar and headed towards Sandy and Ken with a large smile on his face.

"Good news Jimmy?" Ken asked.

"Yeah, Ken. We can have a lie in". He turned and winked at Sandy. She knew that look and raised her empty glass to him.

"Can you get me another one Jimmy darling?"

"Sure, thing love… Ken… another for you?"

"Yeah ta." Ken felt relieved it was good to see him in a better mood. He stood up and said to Sandy,

"I will go and help Jimmy with the drinks."

"Okay."

Up at the bar Ken whispered as discreetly as possible.

"Everything went, ok?"

"Yeah. But… the old sod was about to call the cops when they turned up".

“What!... If this Jake were about to call the police… he must be on to us. Or… Judy could have spooked him. Christ Jimmy what are you going to do?

“I’m not sure yet. I have to think it out. All I know is… I will have to cut off the link between Me and Jake.” He turned and gave Ken a look that Ken had seen before.

“Are the oldies still in one piece?” Ken did not have the stomach for killing.

“Yes, mate they are fine for now.” Jimmy grinned.

As they walked back to the table Ken exhaled with relief as he was following Jimmy, he would not see how relieved he felt.

FOURTEEN

Mary sat weeping as Jake continued to struggle with the ties. He could not re-assure her that they would be alright. As he could not talk. His mouth was getting dry with the gag tied tightly. They had been tied up for a few hours now. It was starting to get dark.

Across the road a short distance away Janet looked out her kitchen window again.

“Clive… they still haven’t turned their lights on.”

“Oh, stop fussing. They have probably gone out for the evening.” Clive was sat in the lounge watching telly.

“Their car is still in the drive.” She had started to worry now.

Clive huffed and spoke

“I suppose you want me to check. They will not thank us for disturbing their evening.” He stood up and went to collect his jacket.

“I’m coming with you.” She bustled about to get her coat on. Janet was a slight woman in her late forties. You would not say she was attractive, although she may have been in her early years. But time had been cruel. In her late twenties she had a miscarriage that triggered a time of depression. It would not take much for her to worry about little things. She had a soft spot for Jake and Mary. They had been friends for several years. Janet would pop over to check if they needed anything and in return Mary turned out to be a good listener. When Janet had a day when she felt a bit low, she would visit Mary and they would talk and eventually end up laughing about something. Clive on the other hand tried his best to understand her mood swings. Most of the time he succeeded. But there were times he wanted to pull his hair out. That would have been a bit awkward as his hair had receded a lot and he ended up with a large bald patch that grew every year. The way it was going, he would be completely bald in his fifties. Not long to go.

They locked up and together walked the short distance to the bungalow where Jake and Mary lived. As they marched up the drive, Janet whispered

"See… their car is parked. I told you."

"Stop fussing will you." Clive was annoyed he was missing a possible goal as he had been watching his favourite football team on the telly playing against their rivals.

They walked up to the front door and rang the bell. No answer…

"See I told you they were out." Clive hissed as he was about to turn and leave.

"I'm going to look in the windows."

"You can't do that."

"Why not if they are out, they will not know will they."

She turned away from the door and carefully made her way through a small flower bed to get closer to the living room window. Her eyes found it difficult to focus as the light was dimming so she could not see much. But as she was about to turn and leave, she caught site of something that made her return to the window. The place looked ransacked.

"Clive…" she called out.

"What?"

"Come here and look."

"What's up?" he was not impressed. He stomped over and protested with every footstep. He looked and had to agree it did look like the place had been ransacked or worse burglars.

"I better check round the back." Clive stepped back and followed the path around the bungalow to the back with Janet closely on his heels. She did not want to be left on her own.

When they got to the back door, nothing looked out of place. Janet still felt uneasy, so she tried the back door.

"Clive…" she whispered.

"The door is not locked."

"Okay, now I am worried." He stepped forward and tried the door and it opened.

"**Jake… Mary… are you there**?" he called out hoping to hear one of them.

Nothing… They listened carefully. Then all of a sudden, they heard muffled sounds. They could not work out what the sounds were.

"Stay here Janet, I'm going in."

"I'm coming with you." She did not take no for an answer and followed him in.

They crept in as quietly as possible. As they neared the living room, they could hear Mary crying. Their pace quickened and they rushed into the room and found the couple tied up and gagged. Janet hurried to Mary to get the gag untied while Clive did the same for Jake.

"Thank you… Thank you…" Jake repeated, his voice barely audible. Then,

"Mary… are you alright my love?" He had tears in his eyes as he struggled to get up to be with her.

Clive suddenly stopped him and guided him to the settee. Then he helped Mary to her feet and sat her next to Jake. They hugged each other.

"Janet… put the kettle on love."

Clive placed his hand on Jakes shoulder for re-assurance.

"Yes of course," she turned back to the kitchen and filled the kettle. She made two cups of tea and gave them to the elderly couple. Mary took hers and almost dropped it through shaking. Luckily, Janet still had hold of the cup and supported it for her. They both took a drink.

"Jake… I am going to call the police." Clive looked around for the phone.

"They ripped it out of the wall." Jake pointed towards the discarded phone lying on the floor. Clive was about to collect it when Janet called out,

"Stop… don't touch anything. We need to leave it as is for the police. Clive can you pop home and call them? I will stay with Jake and Mary."

"Okay love… Jake do you know which door they went out when they left?"

"Um…the front door."

"Right… I will go out the back so if there are any fingerprints, I won't disturb them."

Within ten minutes a Detective John Hirst turned up at the bungalow around 9pm. He was accompanied by a young female PC. They entered the bungalow at the rear as Clive had informed them about the intruder's departure.

"Hello… Jake… Mary…. I am Detective John Hirst, and this is PC Emma Dixon."

Jake was about to try and stand.

"No Jake stay there; you have had a bad experience. Do you need any medical help?"

"No…No, I'm alright, but I am worried about Mary."

"I'm alright Jake. That cup of tea helped, lot of thanks to Janet." She patted Janet's hand affectionately.

"Mrs. Watts… do you have a moment?" Janet stood up and followed Hirst out to the kitchen.

“Thank you for your help, it is Janet?”

“Yes.”

“Janet there is another officer out the front waiting for your statement, a PC Carter. If you could tell him exactly what you did and found here, that would be extremely helpful.”

“What about Mary…”

“Don’t worry the PC will look after her and her husband. We have a doctor coming in to check them over.”

He returned to the living room with a long purposeful stride. A man that commanded respect and there was no doubt he would get it. Although he had control, he also knew how to get the best out of those around him.

“Right… Jake and Mary a doctor will be here shortly just to check you both and then we want to take you somewhere more comfortable. We need to get the forensic team in. Do you have any relatives we can contact?” Hurst enquired.

“No… can we go to Clive and Janet’s? I don’t want to be too far from home.” Jake looked desperate. The Detective glanced to PC Dixon as if to say go check if they can stay with their neighbours. She knew by his look as they had experienced this situation unfortunately many times. So, she left the room and went to speak to Clive and Janet.

Hirst chatted to the couple about general things to keep them as calm as possible, while they waited for the doctor.

After the couple were given all clear, they were taken over the road to Clive and Janet's. Clive had a small office, and this is where the police conducted the interviews. PC Dixon stayed in the lounge with the small group while Hirst took individuals to the office room to question. He knew the quicker they collected data the more accurate the information would be.

He spoke calmly,

"Is it alright I call you Jake?"

"Yes Sir." He sat slightly rigid in the chair.

"Jake…can you, in your own words try and tell me as much as possible what happened this evening?"

Taking a deep breath, he did his best,

"Well, it was around four o clock when the doorbell rang, and Mary went to answer it. I called out who was it. When seconds later I looked up and saw Mary enter, she looked like she was almost running into the living room. I thought what the heck, she does not move that fast normally. Then I realised she had help. A large man wearing a balaclava was pushing her into the room, followed by another man."

"Where they both wearing balaclavas?"

"Yes."

"Carry on... you are doing well. Did they speak?"

"Yes... the one in front barked 'put the phone down' then he shoved Mary into a chair." Jake stopped a moment. Hirst sat waiting not speaking, giving the old man chance to regroup his thoughts. Then Jake continued,

"The one behind, caught hold of the phone and tugged it out of the wall. I asked, 'what do you want, we don't have much'".

"What did they answer?"

"Nothing... they just moved around the room frantically taking anything that took their fancy. The smaller man went over to Mary and just said 'Give.' He had his hand out pointing towards her necklace and rings. I tried to get up to stop him... but the big one barked at me 'Sit.' Then he went to the drawer under where my phone normally sits and emptied it into a bag."

"Did you notice what type of bag he used?"

"Um… I cannot remember, sorry."

"That's alright you have done well."

Jake continued to describe what the men did next like tying them up and just going around knocking things over.

"And then they left as quickly as they came. Mary and I were tied up for several hours… If only we still had Blackie."

"Blackie?"

"Yes, our dog. But he passed away two months ago, we do miss him. If it hadn't been for Clive and Janet…" he tapered off. Hirst knew that Jake had given all the information he could think of and thanked him.

Next, he spoke to Mary. She gave the same account, but she did remember one small detail. The bag was a Tesco's bag. It probably was of no help, but every detail had to be collected.

By around ten-thirty the police had left, and Janet had made up a bed for Jake and Mary. They could not go back to their bungalow until later tomorrow. The Detective told Jake they should be finished sometime tomorrow afternoon, and he ensured that someone would straighten up a bit for them. He added that he would like them to try and make a list of anything missing, but in the morning after they have had a sleep.

FIFTEEN

Tuesday 22nd June

Becky stirred and opened her eyes to bright sunshine. She thought what could be better. Andy was already up. She had not felt him get up and for a moment wondered if he had just popped to the bathroom. No… she could hear him downstairs in the kitchen. She turned on her side and looked at the clock, beside the bed. Eight o clock…

"**Eight o clock**!!" she called out. Jumping out of bed she went to the landing and called out. "**Andy… Why didn't you wake me**?"

"Morning Becky. I thought you looked so peaceful I would let you have a lie in. I am making a coffee; do you want one?"

“Sounds good, I won’t be long.” She went to the bathroom for a quick shower and when she eventually walked into the kitchen, placed on the table was coffee and toast.

“Ooh Andy you are spoiling me.” She sat down to join him.

“You are worth it. Did you sleep well?”

“Yes thanks. I am looking forward to meeting the book club members tonight.”

“Me too.” He took a drink of his coffee, then continued, “I thought I might call Jake today to let him know the journal turned up and to thank him.”

“Good idea.” They finished their breakfast and washed up. As it was still quite early Andy decided to wait a while before calling Jake. He turned to Becky,

“I thought I would call my dad; I feel like I want to know more about why he never knew much about James side of the family.”

“Okay… while you do that, I will put a wash load on.” She pecked him on the cheek and went to fetch the washing. Andy went to the living room and grabbed the phone. He dialled the number and waited for an answer,

“Hello!” a vague answer came.

"Hi mum... it's me Andy. Just thought I would call to check you're both alright."

"Oh, Andy... I didn't recognise the number. It's lovely to hear from you. Are you and Becky settled in now?"

"Yes, thanks mum. Um... mum... is dad about?" I wanted a word."

"Yes love. I will get him."

Moments later a strong male voice came across the phone.

"Hello son, are you both okay?"

"Yeah dad. I wondered if you could help me with something."

"I will try..."

"I was hoping for some luck finding out more about James side of the family." Andy sat with his fingers crossed.

"Well, son... after we last spoke, I went to see your grandad."

"Did you get any more from him?"

"Yes. But only a bit. Not sure if it's much use."

"What was it?"

"Well, it seems that there were a split in the family over William's behaviour."

"What did he do?"

"Well… first of all, I asked your grandad why he could not tell me more before. And he said because of his mum. She was adamant that William did not exist in the family anymore. But now she was gone, he thought he could tell me."

"What on earth did he do?"

"Well… the best way to explain is to tell you from the start. William Keely your grand uncle was born in South Africa. His father worked for the Cullinan Mines. Lawrence and Emily Keely, your great grandparents, lived close to the mine."

William was born 1900 and as Lawrence was in a fortunate position at work, he had a healthy wage.

Lawrence knew his family were privileged compared to the south Africans. After William's birth they decided to return to England. Within eighteen months, William had a sister Matilda.

William went to war and was one of the lucky ones to return. It was whilst he was in the army, he met Kathleen. She worked for the red cross. Their romance blossomed and as William was still quite young, he was easily led. During a night out with some of his fellow army buddies he drank far more than he should. He was a handsome lad, so it was no surprise that he ended up sleeping with a young woman. William felt guilty and vowed he would keep check on his drinking in the future.

About two years later came the day of his wedding to Kathleen. Standing in the church waiting for his bride he felt the luckiest man in the world. The music started and William turned slightly to see her walking down the aisle. She looked stunning and he could not wipe the smile off his face. As she stopped alongside him, she turned back to pass her bouquet to her head bridesmaid. William glanced briefly at the bridesmaid. He went white as a sheet. The family thought William was just feeling nervous.

Kathleen noticed and took his hand.

"Are you alright William?"

"Yes… I am fine." He tried his best to calm down and smiled again.

"After the ceremony Kathleen hugged William and she grabbed his hand and pulled him towards the small group of bridesmaids.

"Darling I want you to meet our bridesmaids."

They had three, two where young girls of twelve and thirteen. Caroline and Audrey and then there was Alice… the same age of Kathleen. William had not met them due to the quick wedding plans as Kathleen was pregnant with James.

Alice turned towards the couple and Kathleen hugged her.

"Alice, meet my lovely new husband, William."

William and Alice politely hugged. Kathleen was about to say more when they were interrupted by a little girl. She came running up to Alice.

"Mummy can I have some cake?" She was around eighteen months to two years old. A little girl with a head full of light blonde curls framing a pretty face.

"Just a minute Molly." Alice scooped her up in her arms.

William stood uncomfortably next to Kathleen in a quiet panic. Alice fortunately focussed on Molly and William's best man

Arthur tapped him on the shoulder. He almost leaped out of his skin.

"Hey mate... didn't mean to make you jump. I just need you for a minute. Ladies can I steal him away?" He grinned and winked at Alice.

"Yes... but not for too long." She laughed.

Later in the early afternoon the small group were mingling and chatting to one another. William sat looking at his beautiful wife Kathleen. She was at the other end of the room talking to her parents and laughing every now and again. He smiled as he watched. Lost in his thoughts.

"Do you have a minute?" a female voice came from behind.

He turned to face Alice.

"Um yes..." he answered cautiously.

"You remember don't you!" she spoke softly.

"Remember... what?"

"So, you're going to play that game. OK... Do you make a habit of getting drunk and taking advantage of innocent girls?" Her face had changed to a determined look.

"I… I… do remember and you were not innocent." He looked at her then at Kathleen.

"Oh, don't worry William, I haven't told Kathleen… yet."

"Don't please she is carrying our baby. It would kill her… please…"

"That's a laugh. I carried our baby on my own and I care for her on my own."

"What… Molly… is mine?" He looked shocked.

"Yes, she is and if you want me to keep quiet, I will need some help financially." She smiled at him as she glanced towards Kathleen.

"I don't have the money." He sounded desperate.

"You may not have money, but I know you have something else you could give me." She winked.

"What… I don't know what you mean."

"When you are drunk you talk a lot."

Back to present day…

"So, you see William was not aware his conversation was overheard by his sister, your nanna. She told your grandad and he said let it be. Well, she never told anyone else in the family apart from your grandad. But she cut William off and his new wife Kathleen was oblivious as to why."

"Oh… so James had a half-sister he never knew of."

"True son. I don't know what happened to her."

"Thanks dad, I will call again soon, love to you both."

Andy placed the phone down and then stood up. He stretched and then went to find Becky.

"Do you fancy a stroll of our estate?" he chuckled.

"Our estate?"

"Yeah… come on, I want to see what we have to tackle to get the grounds up to scratch."

"Okay, I'm going to put on my walking boots as the grass is quite long down that strip."

When they were suitably dressed, they locked up and stood gazing around.

“Where do we start?”

Andy looked towards the barn,

“There…” He pointed to the large building.

“I wonder if there is anything inside?” Becky walked towards the large doors.

“Only one way to find out.” He joined Becky and the pair caught hold of a door and pulled to slide it open. The door was not as heavy as they thought it would be. Tucked in behind the doors they saw some old farm equipment. A meadow plough and a potato planter. There were other smaller implements around on the ground and to one side there were steps leading up to a mezzanine.

“This could be an amazing space to store things for the garden and you could put your car in here.” Becky turned around looking at every nook and cranny.

“Yeah, could do if we move that plough over to the side.”

Becky turned and walked out and took a wander around the outside. To the right of the barn there was an old diesel tank sat on a raised platform. There was evidence of vandalism in the past. The tap broken off in the attempt to remove the tanks contents.

They moved onto the small shed close by, it was a small red brick building with an old wooden door and a tiny window desperately in need of repair. The roof looked reasonably sound, what they could see of it, due to ivy growing over about fifty percent.

"I'm not going in there." Becky stated as she backed away.

"Why not?"

"Because it is probably full of spiders and creepy things." She screwed up her face.

"Alright, I will clean it up a bit later."

"Come on, let's go stretch our legs." She took his hand and they set off down the long run of garden ahead. The light breeze hit their faces as they walked. Becky took a deep breath enjoying the fresh air.

"You know what I need?"

"What?"

"A ride on mower... It would make my job easier, especially this bit." He raised his arm in front indicating the length of land ahead. Becky laughed,

"Well, true... maybe you should."

"Blimey this is a long garden. If you can call it a garden. It is more like a small field."

"Yeah, I wonder what we can do with it?"

"I don't know."

Right at the end of the garden a small hut sat. It had long grass surrounding, apart from the front where the grass had been flattened.

"I'm amazed it's still standing." Becky remarked as she gazed at it.

"It does look a bit fragile." He agreed.

Andy caught hold of the latch on the door and tugged it open. Inside was a small wooden stool and a round little table.

"That's a bit weird. I thought there would be tools in here." He turned to Becky.

"Why just a stool and table?"

"Maybe he had it for solitude to either read or write. I mean, it's peaceful here."

"It sure is." He pulled her into his arms and kissed her cheek, her mouth, then her ear. She hadn't been prepared for such intensity, though she should have been. Everything about Andy was compelling. He held her like the most precious thing in his world. Maybe it was the peaceful atmosphere of the little hut, or the excitement of being outdoors in the elements. They could not stop themselves.

Sandy and Jimmy sat drinking cappuccino in the little café on the Weymouth sea front, she had been to the previous day. Ken had chosen to have a relaxing morning in his room watching some telly. It was around eleven when Jimmy received the call.

"Sorry about this babe… I have to take this." He stood up and walked out into the street to answer it.

"Eddie… my man, where are you?"

"We are about half an hour from you. Where do you want to meet?"

"There is a pub near the sea life centre. I can be there just before twelve and I will get one in for you." He laughed and hung up.

He walked back into the café and re-joined Sandy.

"Is everything alright Jimmy?"

"Yes babes… it could not be better. I'm sitting here with you drinking cappuccino." He picked up his cup and drank.

"What time do we have?... I know that look." She grinned at him.

"Okay caught out. I have to meet someone for work around twelve… sorry love." He leant forwards and kissed her gently.

"She pouted,

"That does not give us long."

"I know love, but I will make it up to you. Come on… drink up."

Reluctantly she did as he requested and stood up to join him. He was at the counter paying. They linked arms and strolled back to the hotel. Sandy set the pace, attempting to get as much time as she could with him. Jimmy would like to have picked up the speed. But, decided to let her have her way this time as all he had on his mind was, he would have the address in his hands soon.

Jimmy and Ken sat in the Brewers Fayre in a corner with drinks, they did not have to wait long. As soon as Jimmy caught sight of the men, he went straight to the bar. Eddie saw him and made a beeline for him with a hand outstretched he shook Jimmy's hand.

"Nice to see you mate, what are you both having?"

“Mines a pint and Ross will have half. He’s driving back.”

The four men sat together in a quiet corner and took large gulps of their drinks.

Eddie placed his glass down on the table and wiped his mouth with his jacket cuff.

“I needed that.”

“Did you have any problems last night?” Jimmy asked.

“Nah… it went like a dream.” Eddie crowed.

“The old biddy made a bit of noise until I shut her up.” Ross was determined to put his pennies worth in.

Jimmy seemed to ignore Ross,

“Eddie, do you have what I need?”

He fished in his pocket and pulled out a little address book. Jimmy took it quickly and immediately thumbed through.

“Ah ha here it is.” He had such a relief rush over his whole body. “This is a good reason for another drink.”

After a negotiation Eddie and Jimmy came to an agreement of payment for the job the previous evening.

“What is so important about that address book?” Ross enquired.

“None of your God dam business.” Came the stern reply that even Ross knew not to continue.

When Eddie and Ross left, Jimmy and Ken went for a walk along the promenade. It was the best way of avoiding any nosey people whilst they discussed the next step.

Meanwhile the police were finishing up at Jake and Marys. Detective Hirst went across the road to collect the elderly couple. He wanted to re-assure them that everything had been set back to its rightful place. Also, to double check on the missing items.

“Can you be sure they never went into any other room?” Hirst looked at the couple intently.

“Definitely not, they did not hang about.” Jake was adamant.

“So, they took your jewellery including rings and watches and emptied a drawer.”

"They also took Jakes wallet." Mary added. She started to weep again.

"Are you sure you want to stay here? Isn't there anyone you could stay with? Just for a few days while you try and recover from your ordeal."

"No... besides, we want to be here to look after our home. We will keep the chains on the doors from now on."

"Good... Oh, your phone is back on."

"Thank you." Jake smiled and said "Tis strange..."

"What?"

"I was about to call you... the police I mean when they barged in."

"Why were you going to ring us?" Hirst's interest peeked.

"Oh... we had a couple of visits that did not sit right with me." He explained the visits and Hirst said that he would ensure a police officer presence for a few days.

"Leave it with me Jake... I will look into it for you." As he left their home, outside, out of earshot he called the station.

"Hirst here… I need a few bodies on patrol near the bungalow."

"Which bungalow Sir?" came the reply.

"The one near Looe, where the assault and robbery took place last night."

"Oh… yes Sir sorry Sir." The young constable on the other end of the phone knew he would be in for an ear bashing on the Detectives return.

SIXTEEN

Tuesday evening

Back in Meadow View, Andy and Becky strolled into the lounge. They had enjoyed the time exploring the grounds and had several ideas on what they could do and would like to do.

Andy decided to look at the journal again. He thumbed through to the page about the book. He read it yet again,

"If you have found 'Stolen' and you are my heir. Then you have started the journey.

But if you are not...then it will be lost for ever...

"I think we need to take this with us to the book club."

"Why? We cannot let others read it... it was James private thoughts."

"True... but if they tell us something of interest, I can add it to his journal."

Becky agreed and suggested they took the book 'Stolen' also. Maybe they could shed a light on why this book was used as a small safe for something."

Andy pulled out of the lane and stopped on the road to wait for Becky. She closed the gate and hopped in the car, and they left for Dorchester, unaware that as they went round the corner another car pulled up by their gate.

"I think this is the place. I will turn round and leave the car in that lay by we passed just now."

"Why can't we drive in there. It is supposed to be empty." Ken inquired.

"Because if someone notices car lights around the place, they could alert the police." Jimmy looked at him and raised his eyebrows. Sometimes Ken could be a bit dim, but he was a loyal trusted friend. Jimmy knew he would always have his back.

They parked up and Jimmy went to the boot to get something solid he could use if needed to gain access to the house. He found the jack handle, what made this a good tool was it was solid and small enough to fit in his pocket. No-good walking down the road with something like a big crowbar. They moved as fast as they could to get back to the gate to get off the road. Climbing over as quickly as possible, they moved through the trees along the lane swiftly.

"It is nice and private here thank god." Jimmy stated.

"Yeah… we shouldn't have an audience."

"We bloody better not." Jimmy whispered.

Although the house was not visible from the road they still went round to the back. Jimmy tried the door.

"Well, you never know." He said hopefully. They both fished in their pockets and pulled out gloves and put them on. Jimmy took the jack handle and hit the glass low down by the door handle. Glass sprayed out everywhere. They quickly gained entry and closed the door behind them. As they did not want to alert any attention, they worked in the dark. It took a few moments to get their bearings and to be able to see a great deal. They went straight through the kitchen and into the hallway. Jimmy whispered,

"You look in that room and I will check this one. You know what you're looking for."

"Yeah... a book called 'Stolen' Cheeky bastard."

Ken hunted through the small room pushing things off the table and piano. Opening cupboard and pulling everything out. While Jimmy did the same in the living room. He came across the phone and decided to do 1471 to see what number came up and he noted it down also checked the re-dial number, noting that one also. He thought maybe it would help if they cannot find the book. He did not know why... but thought he had to cover everything he could think of. He had to get his diamond back.

Nothing found, so, they went upstairs.

“He was a tidy man.” Ken whispered as he entered the main bedroom. He looked around for anything that gave a resemblance of book shaped. He even considered under the bed.

“Yeah… theirs no dust… weird.” Jimmy caught sight of the books on the shelving in the small room.

“Jackpot… Ken come and help me look.”

Ken shot up from the floor and in doing so knocked the bedside cabinet. This in turn knocked the chunky picture flying across the room. He left the room to join Jimmy.

Jimmy ran his finger across bookends looking for the book it was difficult reading the spines in the dark. While Ken just pulled out books and discarded them anywhere. After a thorough search they still could not find it.

“Fuck… Fuck...” Jimmy was fuming.

“It has to be here somewhere.”

“But we have checked everywhere Jimmy.”

“I know…” He ran his fingers through his hair in frustration trying to think of what to do next. They went downstairs and looked again in the rooms hoping they had missed it. On re-entering the kitchen, they stood looking around at everything again. Ken saw some cookery books so, he moved quickly towards them to check through them. The kettle was obstructing the books. So, he reached out to push it out of the way.

"Christ… Jimmy…" he froze.

"What?" He turned rapidly, his pulse quickened, had Ken found it.

"The kettle is warm… the ruddy kettle is warm."

"No… you're imagining it. The old man said he was dead, and the place was empty. Jimmy reached out to touch the kettle.

"Shit…" "We need to get out of here. They moved as fast as possible and fled out to the lane. Keeping as close to the trees they made it up to the gate. Ken was about to climb over when they saw a car approaching. So, he quickly dismounted, and the pair moved under the branches of the trees to hide. Fortunately, the car went by. So, they quickly climbed over the gate and walked briskly to the car. They had learnt by experience not to run as it would attract suspicion if someone were to catch sight of them.

Andy and Becky arrived at Charlie's home and parked in the street under a light. As Andy locked the car, Becky suddenly remembered,

"Andy... you forgot to call Jake."

"Oh yeah I did. I wonder what took my interest elsewhere." He grinned at her and watched her blush.

"I will call him tomorrow morning."

They walked up the tiled pathway to the front door. Moments after ringing the doorbell, the door opened. A large man advanced in years stood in the doorway. A mass of grey hair surrounded by a chubby jolly face.

"Hello... you must be Andy and..."

"Becky." Andy added and stretched his hand out to shake Charlie's.

"Come in and meet the others."

As Becky followed Andy, she could feel butterflies in her stomach. She knew she wanted to be there, but she was still nervous.

The house was welcoming from the moment the door opened to the wide hallway. Upon the walls were the photographs of wildlife, so obviously loved. On the floor stood an old-fashioned parquet with a blend of deep cosy browns and the walls were a soft shade of magnolia. The stair banister was a twirl of wood, controlled by the carpenter's hand, its grain running through as a clematis might, up a trellis. Under the lamp-shine it was nature's art, something that soothed right to the heart. A good first impression.

They walked through the house to the rear, where a large conservatory with several comfortable seats were placed around. There were four men including Charlie.

He was a good host. He showed Becky and Andy to a seat and promptly went around the room introducing each member to the couple. Paul was about six foot tall in his sixties with pepper dash greying hair. A very smartly dressed man. Like an office worker, he was actually a bank manager.

Then there was Peter, a real character. Slightly overweight, he wore glasses that framed his smiling eyes. He was introduced as the joker in the pack. And the final man was Bill, A noticeably quiet thoughtful man.

He was hard to read, he nodded a hello… however he did give a warm smile at the couple.

Charlie poured everyone a drink and they all sat down.

“Firstly. we would like to say how sorry we are to hear of James demise.” Charlie spoke for all as they all agreed.

“Thank you… but as I said to Charlie… I did not know him. This is why Becky, and I accepted your kind invitation tonight. We would love to know more about him.” Andy hardly breathed as he spoke as he was nervous talking to them all.

Paul noticed,

“Andy lad… relax… we don’t bite. You are amongst friends.”

“Thank you.”

“Are either of you interested in books?” Paul asked.

“Yes… I have always loved them. So, I was surprised to see James collection.” Becky had plucked up the courage to speak and it seemed to relax everyone in the room.

Charlie announced.

“Let us see if we can help our young couple with something we knew about James. I will start... He was very punctual. It was one of his pet hates... being late. Oh... and he treated his books with a lot of love.”

Paul was next,

“James had a good sense of humour. I remember one time when he brought some books, he had acquired from a book sale down in Cornwall. He brought several hardbacks and placed them on the table in the middle of the room. We all went to pick one to check over and I had a bit of a surprise. I picked up a book and I could see James had a twinkle in his eye, but did not give it too much attention until... I opened the book and found the whole book was upside down.”

“What do you mean upside down?” Andy asked.

“The book was one way and the cover another... you may think that’s not funny... but not until you read the title. ‘The World turned upside down’. James had changed the cover just to see my reaction.”

Bill spoke next, a man of few words,

“James was very picky with his books. He treated them with respect and would frown on others that didn’t.”

Peter sat rubbing his chin.

“Well… what can I say, he wasn’t a handsome chap like me.” He laughed.

“No seriously. He was a good bloke. Always ready to help any of us if we needed anything.”

Charlie looked around the room as if to say is it okay if I add something. The group nodded and he spoke.

“Andy… Becky… is there anything you would like to ask us?”

Andy looked at Becky for a second, then, he replied.

“Um… I wonder if any of you has seen this book before?” Becky fumbled in her bag and pulled out the hardback book ‘Stolen’. She passed it to Andy. He held it up and then passed it to Charlie.

Charlie’s face looked puzzled as the weight was not what he expected. So, he opened it.

“Christ almighty… What’s happened here?” He held the book up to show the others. For a moment, the room went silent. Then they all seemed to talk at once.

“Who the hell did that?” Bill asked. Whilst Paul asked.

“Is it a book safe?”

The room went silent again, as they all turned to Paul and stared at him questioning.

“What?... I did not do it. I’ve never seen that book before.” He raised his hands in defence.

Andy quickly stepped in,

“Oh… we are not saying any of you did it. But… would James have done it?”

“Definitely not.” Bill came back quickly in protection of his old friend.

“Let me explain.” Andy started.

“Becky was sorting James books and came across this one amongst the piles. We both thought it was a strange find. I even rang his friend Jake from Looe to ask about it. And like you, he said that no way would James deface a book.”

Paul had a sudden thought,

“Andy… was there anything hidden inside?”

"No."

"Have you seen anything like this before?" Becky asked, then continued,

"Only you recognised it extremely quickly."

"I have seen book safes before. But not so crudely made. Sometimes a customer will bring one in with precious things inside to put in a safety box."

"Oh... I didn't know they still had safety boxes."

"Yes Becky, but only a few banks offer this facility. We do not have many though, only about a dozen." He turned to Charlie,

"Can I have a closer look at it?"

"Yeah course." He passed the book to Paul.

As he studied the insides he commented,

"It looks like it was made in a hurry."

"I wonder what was hidden in it." Charlie surmised.

They spent the rest of the evening as they would normally at the book club. And both Becky and Andy enjoyed the banter between the group about the books they had read that previous month. As they were about to leave, the book club asked if they would like to join.

“What does it entail?” Andy asked.

“All we ask is for you to agree holding the meeting when it is your turn. Oh, and if you have time to read a book a month. Then we have another title to discuss.” Charlie looked at the pair in anticipation for an answer. Andy could see Becky was keen. So, they agreed, but Andy said,

“I expect it will be Becky doing the reading, as I am a slow reader if that is okay?”

“Sure thing, we are not sexist here.”

Andy and Becky said their goodbyes and left; They drove home to Meadow view. Andy pulled up to the gate and Becky got out to open it. He drove through and she closed the gate. When they got out of the car Becky placed her arm over Andy’s shoulder and said rather sleepily,

“I enjoyed tonight, but I am tired.”

“Me too.” He hugged her then opened the front door. Becky stepped into the hallway. She shivered.

“Cor it’s cold in here. There is a draft somewhere!”

"You are right... it is. I will go and put the kettle on." He passed her as she went into the front room.

"**Becky… Becky…**" He called.

"What is it, Andy?" She dragged herself off the settee and entered the kitchen.

"Oh no! Andy…" she felt tears prickling in her eyes as she looked at the back door.

"Well, we know where the draft has come from. Don't touch anything. I will call the police."

Becky just stood frozen in shock, she muttered to herself,

"Christ… what if someone is still in the house." Panic took over and she ran into the living room as Andy replace the phone. She whispered.

"Andy… what if they're still in the house!"

"Oh crap… I had not thought of that. Come on… he grabbed his car keys and her hand and led her quickly out to the car. They got in and locked the car doors and waited for the police.

Andy and Becky sat huddled together in the car waiting for the police to arrive. Fortunately, they did not have to wait too long. When the police car drove up to the house, Andy and Becky got out and walked up to it. Very quickly they brought the police up to date on the details of what they found and did.

One officer asked them to stay with the car, while he and his colleague went to check out the property.

About five minutes later they returned and asked the couple to come back to the house. They assured them there was no one in there.

Back in the kitchen one of the officers asked Andy to follow him around to confirm if he could see anything missing. Becky went and put the kettle on and offered to make a drink for the officers. They accepted her offer gladly. They had a long shift through the night ahead. Andy followed the officer around the house downstairs and could not see anything untoward, apart from things flung around rooms. So, they headed upstairs. Within seconds Andy noticed the small room where the books were kept.

"Oh no..."

"What is it?"

“Someone has been pulling out the books. Becky had just sorted those and made a good job. She will be gutted.”

“Did you have anything else on the shelves apart from books?”

“No… oh they have made an awful mess.” He was about to pick up a book when the officer stopped him.

“We will need to check for fingerprints. But to be honest as you cannot see anything missing, I reckon it were teenagers just entering to make a mess. It could have been a lot worse.”

It did not make Andy feel any better. A few hours later the police left, and Becky and Andy sat to the kitchen table with a hot drink, they were mentally exhausted. The back door boarded up and secure. Andy took hold of his mug and drank the last of his drink. He pushed his chair back and stood up.

“Come on love, let’s get to bed, we need sleep. In the morning I will get onto the alarm people and see if they can come sooner than they intended.”

Becky yawned and slowly got up.

"Yeah, that's a good idea and we need to clean the whole house again." She took her mug to the sink and placed it in the bowl and was about to run some water to wash the cups when Andy placed an arm over her shoulder and tenderly whispered in her ear. "Leave them… come on, bedtime." And he pulled her gently away and led her upstairs.

SEVENTEEN

Wednesday 23rd June

In Cornwall and Devon police headquarters in Austell, Taylor was not in a happy mood. And when he was unhappy, he made sure others felt the same.

"Come on you lot… someone must be missing a mum, sister or wife." His voice filled the room, and everyone stopped what they were doing. They waited for the next explosion. They knew it was coming.

"Surely one of you has something on her... **Well!"** He became redder in the face with every word.

No one answered.

"**For Christ's sake... someone get onto forensics and get me something."**

It was Sergeant Wheely that left the room in search of the forensics report. Around ten minutes later he returned with the report and passed it to Taylor. He held the paper and went down a check list.

Fingerprints – blank

Dental analysis – blank she had false teeth.

Attached to the paper was a photo of the woman. Not a good one, as the face had been disfigured by birds and other creatures. Not a pretty sight.

All they could get from her was, she had been strangled and that she wore a dressing gown and underwear. She had bare feet that had no marks from being outside walking. So, they could surmise she had been killed inside and brought to this destination and dumped. A horrible way to end one's life. They could estimate she was in her late fifties maybe early sixties, and she had mousey short hair. She was five feet two and overweight. As they could not use her photo, they called in a police artist to draw a likeness as she would have been. They were going to use it on the television statement that evening in hope of getting someone to come forward and identify her.

Back in Meadow View

Although they had not slept as well as they wanted both Andy and Becky were up early. They wanted to clean the house from top to bottom as soon as possible. It felt like they had been violated. The Police had collected all they required and had promised they would inform them of any progress if they had any other reports of other break-ins. But as they could not get many fingerprints, they did not hold any luck. They had taken Andy and Becky's to eliminate.

Andy made a call to the security firm and the soonest they could fit them in would be in two days. He was incredibly grateful and the next call he made was to a glazier to get the back door repaired. They would be with them around eleven.

Becky was in the kitchen washing up the breakfast dishes when Andy walked in and announced he had sorted the two jobs required to help get the house more secure.

“Andy… we ought to call Jake again, we did promise to.”

“Yeah, true and it would be good to hear his cheery voice. I do like him. We will have to go and visit him one day soon.”

“I like the idea of that.” She smiled and dried her hands as they both entered the living room to call him.

“Andy lad, it is good to hear from you.” Jake seemed extremely pleased to hear from them.

“I hope it is not too early to call.”

“No lad, we do not sleep in. Us old ones seem to wake earlier nowadays. Before I forget, can you give me your phone number?”

Andy looked puzzled,

“Um yeah… I thought you had it.”

“Well, Andy, I did have it written in my address book, but it was stolen.”

“Oh my god… when?”

“A couple of days ago.”

"How come?"

Jake went through the events of that day.

"Are you both alright?" Andy sounded concerned and Becky was desperate to know what was wrong. She was fidgeting in her seat. Andy mouthed he would tell her as soon as he came off the phone.

"Yes, lad we are, the police have been really good to us."

"It is weird you had someone taking your belongings. Because last night while we were out, we had a break in."

"Did they get much?"

"No… in fact we could not see that anything was taken. But they made a mess of James books."

"I have a nasty feeling about all of this happening."

"What do you mean? Andy looked confused.

"Well… I feel all what is happening is linked with this ruddy book of Danny's that James bought from Lily."

“Do you think it was a first edition? Because that is what would make a book worth a lot of money.”

“Could be… but James was astute and if he had found a first addition, he would have contacted Lily straight away. He had the last box of books from Lily around easter and when he came down just before Christmas, he never said anything to me.”

“Did he mention the book with the cut-out papers?”

“Come to think of it… we did have a strange conversation one time. He asked what Lily did for a living and when I said she had not worked for some time as her brother Danny looked after her above his jewellers. I do remember he went quiet after that.”

“Strange!” Andy chatted for a while longer with Jake and asked if they could come and see them one day soon. Jake sounded extremely happy with this idea.

When Andy got off the phone, he relayed the conversation to Becky.

“Andy… I think Jake might be right. Whatever is happening it is to do with that flaming book. Do you think there was something valuable hidden inside?”

“I do… but what? And more so where is it now?”

In Saltash Police Station, Hirst looked over the interview details that Jake and Mary had given him. It troubled him greatly. An elderly couple in their own home, being attacked like that, what was the world coming to. He stood up from his desk and went to his office door and called.

"PC Dixon… do you have a moment?”

“Yes Sir…” Dixon moved swiftly to his door and tapped once.

“Come in.”

She entered and stood in front of his desk waiting for his request.

“Sit down Emma… I want to go over a few things about the assault and robbery case in Looe.”

She stepped forward and sat on the chair to the left front of the desk. Emma was happy in her job, so much so, that when asked if she would like to further her career, she quickly explained that she wanted to stay in the same position as a PC. She sat perched on the chair waiting for Hirst to speak.

"Emma… I want to go through some of the statements we took from Jake and Mary."

"Yes sir." As she was a petite woman, she caught hold of her chair at the front of the seat and edged it slightly closer to his desk, so she could see the notes better.

"I see in your notes that you spoke with Mary at some length. Can you go through it again with me?"

"Sure… Mary was quite distressed, but she was very clear on some of her facts." Emma picked up her notes and read.

"Mary insisted we check into the woman from Liskeard Hospital."

"Woman…" he interrupted.

"Yes, it seems that the couple have had two previous visits before this attack."

"Yes, Jake told me of the two men enquiring about some book." He stopped to shuffle through his papers.

"Ah… here it is… Now… I will concentrate on the two men. Can you check out this woman? Oh… before you go to the hospital, can you re-visit Mary and Jake to see if they remember a name for this woman and a description."

"Will do sir."

"Thank you. Let me know what you find."

"Yes sir." She stood up and left the room. Hirst smiled affectionately as he watched her leave. He knew he could rely on her when it came to gathering details in a case. She might be small in stature five feet, but her mind was not, she was very bright.

Emma pulled up in front of the bungalow and was happy to see a police presence. She felt they needed protection. Something did not sit right with her. She could not put her finger on it. But when Emma had this feeling, she knew she could not let it go until she had all the details in order.

She was just about to tap the door when it opened, and Jake stood smiling at her. He welcomed her in, and Mary insisted she had a cup of tea,

Once Mary had brought the tea through to the living room and settled with her cup Emma started to chat with the couple. First of all, she asked if they had got any sleep and if there were anything they needed.

“I did try and sleep, but I got a few hours. My Jake is a sweetie, he brought me a drink around six this morning and we have been just resting today.”

“You have a good husband, Mary.” She turned slightly and winked at Jake.

“I cannot complain either, we are a good team aren’t we dear.” He reached across and squeezed her hand affectionately.

Emma gave them a moment. Then she asked,

“Do you mind going over the day a woman came to ask about your friend James?”

Jake spoke first.

“Aye… She turned up a couple days ago out of the blue, she said she were from the hospital in the offices. Something about belongings left by James, she wanted his address. I must admit I was a bit rude to her.”

“Why was that?”

“Well… I do not know. But I had a gut feeling that she was not all that she made out to be. I mean, when would a hospital come all the way out to visit a friend of the deceased to get information. They would maybe ring, or… call the coroner for details of contact about James."

"You are astute Jake; you should come and work with us." She joked.

"Sorry… joking apart, I want you both to think hard. Did this woman give you a name?"

Jake and Mary looked at one another and shook their heads.

"Okay don't worry. Can you describe her please?"

Jake answered again,

"She was very smart in appearance, and I would say she were around her early forties or late thirties. Mind you I am no good with age."

"I thought she was a lovely lady, very polite and well spoken. Although she did seem a bit nervous." Mary added.

"Aye… that's why I was not so sure on her telling the truth. It's like I told Mr. Willis…"

"Willis… who is Mr. Willis?" Emma's ears pricked up and she felt a spark of interest.

"Oh, sorry miss… Mr. Willis is one of James Solicitor. Or I should say he was."

“Just a minute… can you please explain why you told this Mr. Willis about the young woman’s visit?”

Jake seemed to enjoy explaining. He went through the details again about the phone calls and co-incidences with his request from the hospital and the solicitors same request, but by a man.”

Emma felt the excitement build up in the pit of her stomach. She seemed to know when there were good leads presenting themselves.

The phone rang and Mary jumped it was obvious she was not herself yet.

“Oh, excuse me a moment. I will just see who it is, and I can call them back.” Jake moved to the phone before Emma could say anything. She was about to leave, but now she had to wait until Jake finished on the phone. So, she turned her attention to Mary.

“Are you okay Mary?” she could see Mary looked a little wary.

“Yes dear… it is silly… but any sudden noise or movement and I jump like a jack rabbit.” She tried to brush it off with a slight chuckle.

"You are not silly at all. You both went through a nasty experience."

In the background she heard a one-sided conversation on the phone.

"Hello, Mr. Willis...yes, I'm sorry.... Well, you see we could not answer the phone because it had been ripped out of the wall...We had a couple of unwanted visitors. Two men." There was a slightly longer silence as George Willis spoke. Then Jake replied,

"I did not get the chance to call them. But we do have a PC Dixon here at the moment." He turned slightly to glance at the two women. "Sure... just a moment. PC Dixon... Mr. Willis would like a word." Jake passed the phone to her.

"Hello Mr. Willis, PC Dixon..." she waited for a reply.

"PC Dixon... are Mary and Jake alright?" he sounded very anxious.

"Yes, they are fine. A bit shaken though."

"I am genuinely concerned for their safety. There is something not right about this whole business."

"I know what you mean, may we call you later if required?

"Of course, Jake can give you, our number."

"Thank you, oh, and please do not worry, we have our team keeping an eye on your friends." She passed the phone back to Jake.

When he got off the phone, she asked for George Willis phone number.

"Yes … I will get it for you… Oh my goodness I cannot, my address book with phone numbers were taken."

"Please do not worry, I can get his number when I return to the station."

She thanked the couple and left for Liskeard Hospital.

Emma entered the hospital and went to the reception desk. It took a while to get through to the young girl who she needed to talk to. But eventually a middle-aged man arrived at the desk to see if he could help her.

"PC Dixon?" he enquired, as he stretched out a hand to greet her.

"Yes."

"I am Stephen Jenkins; how can I help you?" he gave a well-practiced smile.

“Is there somewhere we can go that is more private?”

“Um yes.” He was taken back at her request. It sounded a bit ominous. He led her down a long corridor and they entered a door on the right with a name plate private.

“Take a seat… now how can we help you?” he asked as he sat the other side of a small desk.

“I need to ask if you sent a woman to a friend of a deceased for their address.”

“What do you mean? Sent…”

Dixon explained the visit and request. He looked surprised, but he fired up the computer on the desk and after obtaining James name, brought up his details.

“Hmm… we have his address, so, we would not send someone out to obtain it. To be honest if we did need it, we would contact his next of kin. But in James case the next of kin was unknown. So, we would have spoken to the person that called us in the first place.”

“Thank you for your help. I must admit I thought it was a strange thing to do. Can I ask you something else?”

“Sure.”

"We were informed that the hospital recently received a call from James solicitor Mr. Willis, enquiring about a man that was supposed to work in your office trying to get James address."

"Oh, I see. I am afraid I have not been told he called. But it does seem a strange co-incidence."

When Emma returned to the station, she went straight to report back to Hirst.

"How did you get on?" he asked as she entered and sat down in the chair by the desk again.

"Pretty good Sir. I feel we were right to check out the hospital." She relayed all the information she had gathered.

"Well done. I will leave you to call this solicitor Emma."

She spoke to George Willis on the phone.

"Mr. Willis, thank you for your time."

"How can I help you?"

"We need an address of a late client of yours."

"Oh yes… who?"

"A James Keely…"

"I see… can I ask why?"

"I cannot go into too much detail, but… is his property empty?"

"No… He had a relative that has just moved in with his partner."

"I see sir. We are to believe they may be in danger."

"Oh, my goodness!"

"Please do not worry it is speculation at the moment. But we need to contact them."

"Of course. Give me a moment and I will get you their address and contact number." He put the phone down briefly while he went to the files and pulled out the details.

"Do you have a pen P C Dixon?"

"Yes… fire away." She scribbled down the details and thanked him for his help.

"You are welcome, is there anything else I can help you with?"

"No… Oh… there is one thing… do not call Andrew Randle about this. We will send someone from Dorchester police station to put them in the picture. It is a delicate situation that our offices are trained to deal with. No offence meant sir."

"None taken."

Dixon went to Hirst's office and tapped on the door.

"Enter."

"Sir I have the details you required… the address of an Andrew Randle. He is a relative living at James Keely's old house."

"Where is it?"

"A little hamlet called Druce in Dorset."

"Oh… I think I need to call Detective Alan Thomas at Dorchester station."

"Yes Sir… will that be all?"

"For the moment… thank you Dixon."

She turned and left the office to catch up on some other work. While Hirst, grabbed the phone and made a call.

It was late Wednesday afternoon.

"Detective Alan Thomas please…"

The voice on the other end enquired

"Who should I say is calling?"

"Detective John Hirst of Saltash Police station."

"Yes sir, I won't be a moment."

Seconds later the voice of Alan Thomas spoke,

"Hello John, it has been a long time. How are things down there?"

"Alan it's good to hear you. I am hoping you can help me with a small problem."

"I am sure I can... tell me about it."

Hirst explained the situation and brought him up to speed.

"I see what you mean. So, you expect these men to come over to Dorset in search of a book... There has to be more to it."

"I know... that's what I think. By all accounts the young couple living at Meadow View are unaware of this going on. Do you have a female P C that is good at keeping things calm?"

"Yeah, I have just the right person, she's not a P C, she is a Sargent. Sargent Peggy Collins... she is good at putting people at their ease. I will accompany her as well. I will report back to you once we have made contact."

"Thanks Alan, really appreciate it."

Alan Thomas put the phone down and went to the door of his office. He called for Peggy.

"Come in Peggy." He beckoned her in.

"Yes Gov, ... How can I help?"

"Take a seat... we have a task to complete that could be a bit awkward and I need your expert help."

She sat intrigued.

"Sounds interesting".

Alan Thomas explained the situation and gave Peggy a moment.

"I see what you mean. The thought of two unsavoury thugs coming in on our patch is not something I relish. But worse still is, we have a young couple oblivious of the possible danger they may be in."

Alan pushed his chair back and stood up and grabbed his jacket.

"Are you ready?"

“Yes Gov, … I think the sooner we put these people in the picture the better.”

They spoke as they walked through the station towards the entrance door.

“Yes … and I will put a small surveillance team on them for a while to be safe.”

“Where do they live?”

“A place called Meadow View, Druce.” Alan held the main door open for Peggy.

“Excuse me Sir…” A PC had just entered the station when he overheard the address.

Alan stopped in his tracks.

” Yes, what is it?” he had turned looking a bit agitated due to the fact he wanted to get on.

“May I ask, are you going to Meadow View?” The PC stood a little nervous asking a Detective a question.

“Yes lad… Why?”

“Well… PC White and I were out there last night dealing with the break in, and I wondered if I could help… Sir.” He trailed off thinking it had been a stupid idea.

D. I. Thomas stood still a moment, then asked, “PC…Keen… isn’t it?”

“Yes Sir…” He stood waiting to be reprimanded… instead…

“Keen, can you spare me a couple of hours?”

“Yes Sir… I just need to let the desk know and I can be with you in a jiffy.”

“Good man. Meet me out in the car park as soon as possible, my car is the dark grey BMW.”

“Yes Sir.”

As PC Keen turned away to speak to the desk sergeant he had a small grin on his face, he had not got a reprimand like he thought he would, instead he would be working alongside Detective Alan Thomas he was the youngest police officer that achieved Detective status and had a good reputation. PCs were queueing up to get noticed and have the opportunity to work on his team. So even if it were just for one day PC Keen would take it gladly.

EIGHTEEN

Meanwhile in Weymouth, Jimmy sat in the Range Rover with Ken in the hotel car park. It was the morning after the attempt to retrieve the book with the diamond.

“What do we do now Jimmy?” Ken was unsure at asking this question in fear of Jimmy getting riled up and doing something bad, but he wanted to know.

“Fuck knows… I reckon we need to visit this relative that is living in the house and ask a few questions.”

“Like what?”

“What the fuck have they done with my diamond.” With a look as black as thunder Jimmy turned the key and pulled out of the car park.

Ken sat quietly beside him thinking how I can calm him down and most of all how are we going to ask the question. After a short while he suddenly had a thought.

Cautiously he asked,

"Jimmy… do you have Jake's address book with you?"

"Yeah… why?"

"Well, maybe there is more contact numbers and addresses for this James in Dorset. Like a number to call if he cannot get James in an emergency."

Jimmy turned his head and smiled.

"See I knew why I brought you with me. Who's a clever lad. "He reached out and patted Ken on the shoulder.

At the next lay by they saw, Jimmy pulled in.

He turned off the engine and went to his pocket and pulled out the small address book. He thumbed through page by page until he found James address again. Running his finger down the page he saw a note beneath James address. Deceased Andy Randell.

'If urgent to reach James, call Charlie'.

"Ah ha… well done Ken. Now who is this, Charlie?"

"Doesn't it say."

"No mate… Blast it." He spent the next five minutes checking through the list of names.

He found two Charlies in Dorset. One a Charlie Black, His address was Flat 1A above The Fancy Friers, Trinity Street, Dorchester, Dorset. And the other one was a Charlie Booker, 27 Prince of Wales Road, Dorchester, Dorset.

"So, which one is it?" Ken asked.

"I have no idea."

They sat for a moment thinking what to do when Jimmy thought of something.

"I think we could try out the fish and chips at the Fancy Frier. At least we would have a good reason for entering the property."

"Sounds good to me."

Jimmy started the engine, and they re-joined the traffic and travelled to Dorchester. They parked in the top of town car park again as they would know where they left the car. They walked down the high street towards the centre of town, they passed Willis and Banks Solicitors. Jimmy noticed and grunted...

"Awkward bastard..." Then continued on pass towards the Horse with the Red Umbrella tea shop. They realised it was on the corner of Trinity Street the street they wanted. So, they turned in and walked and walked. Eventually nearing the other end of this road, they found the Fancy Frier on their left. Right opposite was a car park.

"Crap, Jimmy, we could have parked there and just crossed the road."

"Stop moaning Ken, the walk has built up your appetite."

"I could still eat fish and chips without all that walking. And worse still, it is up hill on the way back."

"Then after you have eaten your chips, you will have the energy to walk it, won't you?" He turned and grinned.

They walked into the Friers and ordered fish and chips twice. As they waited for them, Jimmy noticed an A4 framed piece of paper on the wall with the name of the proprietor on it He nudged Ken and whispered,

"Look at that… proprietor Mr Charlie Black."

Ken smiled and Jimmy casually spoke to the man behind the counter as he filled the second bag with chips.

"I don't suppose I could speak to the proprietor?"

"Speaking… what can I do for you?" he looked up and smiled at Jimmy.

"Well, that's a bit of luck isn't it mate."

He nudged Ken and quickly Ken nodded in agreement, not knowing what Jimmy was on about. But he knew to agree straight away. Jimmy continued,

"You see our friend James told us about your great fish and chips and said if we got to come to Dorchester, we had to try them. He also said to say hello to you from him."

"James?" he looked confused,

"I don't know a James, what's his surname?"

"Keely..." Jimmy looked hopeful it would jog his memory.

"Sorry mate, never heard of him. But I am sure you will enjoy our fish and chips. We pride ourselves in making the best in Dorset." He gave a huge smile as he passed them to Jimmy.

He took them and had to force a thank you smile as he turned for the door. Inside he was fuming.

They ate their fish and chips as they walked back to the car and to be honest Charlie was correct. The food was good. They finished their chips standing in the carpark, as Jimmy would not have the smell of fried food in the car. Ken found a waste bin and disposed of the wrappers. Luckily, there were toilets in the car park, so they were able to relieve themselves and wash their hands before getting back in the car.

“Now what Jimmy?”

“Christ, I don’t know.”

Jimmy got the address book again and found Charlie Bookers address and tapped it in the sat nav. He started the car up and they pulled out of the car park and turned left. At the roundabout they turned right and followed the road until they came to traffic lights. They had to stop at a red light.

“We are not going into this Charlies place in broad daylight, are we?”

“No Ken, course not.” He noticed the lights turning and pulled away and turned left. At the end of the road, they turned left again and then took the second right into a road that led to the Prince of Wales Road. The car crawled along slowly as they looked for number 27. The road was adorned by beautiful, detached houses, some with grand gardens.

“Cor looks like a wealthy area.” Ken observed.

"Yeah... sure is. Keep your eyes open for the numbers."

"Will do... stop!"

"Have you seen it?!

"Yeah... it's the one on the left." He pointed out a red brick Edwardian house.

"Right... remember which house it is, so we can find it later."

Ken quickly glanced around and noticed a small post box opposite. Jimmy drove past the house looking around the place as much as he could. He continued up the road until he came to a side street where he turned round and drove back down. As he neared the house again, he slowed.

"**Dam and blast it."** He shouted.

"What Jimmy?"

"He has a high-end burglar alarm system."

"So, What now?"

"We go back to the hotel and work out a plan. Then get drunk." He sounded really despondent.

Meanwhile, Detective Thomas and Sergeant Collins sat in the car waiting for PC Keen. It looks as though our men from Cornwall may have visited already."

The back door of his BMW opened, and PC Keen got in.

"Keen… this is Sergeant Collins, buckle up."

"Mam…" he acknowledged politely.

"Keen… So, tell us about this break in."

"To be honest… it looked like it could have been kids breaking in to mess up the place."

Alan interrupted,

"Did they mess up really bad?"

"No sir… just certain places. The worst was a small bedroom."

"Bedroom!" Peggy was intrigued.

"Yes mam… the room had bookshelves, and someone had pulled out most of them and thrown them."

"Strange…" Alan murmured as he drove.

It was not long when they arrived at Meadow View. He had rung beforehand to ask if it was okay for a visit. Obviously, Andy had agreed, as he thought it was to be an update on the attempted burglary. Alan had thought it strange that Andy had not queried their visit. Still, they were here now. Parked up and standing out by the car Thomas announced. “Right PC Keen I need you to just observe for the moment unless I ask for your input. “

“Yes Sir.”

Peggy knew the way Alan worked so she did not need instructions. Alan Thomas was very astute in the way he conducted his interviews. They walked up to the front door and rang the bell.

Becky answered it moments later and was taken back to see three police stood there.

Detective Alan Thomas held up his card and introduced everyone to Becky before she invited them in. She showed them to the living room and as they settled down on one of the settees, Andy walked in to join them. Thomas raised from his seat to greet Andy.

“Please take a seat… would anyone like a drink?” He looked from left to right and it was Collins that spoke first.

“A juice would be lovely if that’s okay.”

Becky answered

“Sure… anyone else?”

It was like the flood gates had opened, Thomas had nodded

“the same please” and PC Keen agreed also to have one.

Becky went to get them, whilst Andy took a seat opposite the officers.

“So, is there some news on our break in?”

Thomas answered,

“Not yet Andy… but shall we wait for Becky before we continue?”

“Yeah… okay.” Andy looked a bit baffled but smiled weakly and they sat in silence.

Becky walked in with a tray full of drinks. She placed it down on the table and passed the glasses around. Andy was the first to speak, asking…

“So, do you have any news on who broke into our home?”

“Sorry Andy, not yet. PC White has brought me up to speed on your break in. We are certainly going to look into this for you.” Thomas assured them.

“Isn’t it a bit overkill… Sorry… I mean sending a detective, Sergeant and PC to deal with a break in? I mean nothing was taken." Becky looked at Detective Thomas as she spoke.

"Well, Becky... you are astute I can say that." He smiled and then continued.

"You see, Andy and Becky... we will look into your burglary naturally... But there is something else we need to discuss with you." He paused for a moment.

"What!" Andy sat forward to listen more intently.

"We are here to speak about Jake and Mary..."

Before he could add anything, Becky interrupted,

"Oh my God... are they alright?"

"Yes, Yes... they are fine. Our colleagues are keeping them safe don't worry."

Collins moved towards Becky just in case she needed to comfort her. But Becky was made of stronger stuff.

"Then what is it?" Andy was getting concerned.

Thomas kept his voice calm and steady, "Jake has informed my colleagues he had a visit from two men. These men unsettled him." Thomas was about to continue when Andy interrupted,

"I know about these men, Jake told me a few days ago."

"What did he say?" Thomas thought he may have given Andy more detail than they had.

"Well, not a lot... but he did say he didn't trust them and that they may try and find our home."

"Why would they want to find your home in particular?" Thomas asked curiously.

"He said they were after a book and that it may be at our place."

"A book?" Collins could not resist asking.

Andy did his best to explain the whole conversation he had with Jake and also added that he, Andy should not deal with them and keep far away if possible.

"Well Andy and Becky... it looks like they have already tried to retrieve the book already. Do you, have it?"

"I'm not sure. I mean for a book to be valuable it would have to be a first addition, wouldn't it?"

"Maybe..." Thomas pondered.

"It could be 'Stolen'..." Becky looked at Andy.

"I thought you said nothing was taken."

Andy and Becky looked at one another as if to have a conversation in their heads, 'should we tell them or not!!

Andy nodded, so Becky stood up and went for her bag. Before she delved into it... Andy announced...

"Becky was right Detective... nothing was stolen. What she is on about is a book with the title 'Stolen'".

All three police officers were sat baffled.

"Please explain..." Thomas asked.

"Well, while Becky was sorting and tidying the books in the little bedroom, she came across a book. The title... 'Stolen'." Andy continued to explain what was so unusual about the book. Then Becky pulled it out of her bag. She passed it to the detective and waited. He opened the book and just stared at it for a while.

"Was there anything in the book hidden?"

"No..." both Becky and Andy answered together.

Thomas thought for a moment, then asked, “Can I take the book? to test for fingerprints.”

“Um… yes. But it will have ours on it and I suppose James.” Andy passed it towards the detective. But he did not take it before he had taken a plastic bag from his pocket and Andy dropped it in.

“Thank you. We will return it to you as soon as possible.”

Suddenly Becky said

“Oh, Detective Thomas there will be other fingerprints from the book club.”

“The book club!” he questioned.

“Yes, we took it to the book club the night we were broken into.”

” Ah, I see, thank you. We will see how many clean prints we get first and if required we will call for more details.”

Andy turned to PC Keen and asked,

“PC Keen, did you get any prints from the break in?”

He looked towards Thomas waiting for the consent to answer the question. Thomas nodded and he replied,

“We were only able to collect one from the back door handle.”

“Well, one is better than none.” Andy tried to sound optimistic.

“Very true Andy, My team will get onto it as quickly as possible. In the meantime, we would like to place a small team around your property just for a while. It is just a contingency to help you feel safe.”

“Thank you, detective.” They shook hands as the small group stood.

“We will be in touch and if you have any concerns or think of anything that may help, please call me.” Thomas handed Andy a small card with his contact details. As they were about to leave Andy called after Detective Thomas,

“Um it may not be anything…”

“What Andy?”

“Well, if you could talk to Lily, she may be able to help.”

“Who is Lily?”

“She is the person that sold James the book.”

"Very true Andy. Do you know where she is?"

"No... I don't but maybe Jake has heard from her."

"Thank you, Andy."

Then they left.

As they travelled back to the station Thomas said,

"I want all you have on this break in, including the fingerprints. Oh, and Keen, you will be working on my team while we get to the bottom of this."

"Yes Sir." Keen sat in the back doing his best not to show a huge smile that appeared on his face. He was a bright young PC. His dream was to work his way up to a murder squad. So, this would be a step in the right direction, as Detective Thomas had an extremely good reputation and better still, he achieved a high clear up rate.

NINETEEN

Thursday 24th

Alan Thomas picked up the phone and called John Hirst.

"Hello Alan, how did you get on with the young couple?"

"Pretty good." He went through the details including their break in and finished off with the suggestion to contact this Lily.

"Sounds good to me. I am up for trying a new avenue to get to the bottom of this whole ruddy puzzle. I will visit Jake and Mary again."

" let me know how you get on."

"Will do."

Around 10 30 a m. Hirst and Dixon arrived at Jake and Mary's home again. Jake opened the door and gave them a broad smile. "Come in… Mary will be pleased to see you."

"How is she today?" Dixon asked as they stepped in through the front door.

"Oh, she's getting there. Mary… we have visitors, put the kettle on love."

From the kitchen they heard a cheery reply, and they entered the living room.

After they all settled down with a hot cup of tea, Hirst gradually started to question the couple.

"Jake… you told me about the two men that visited you… and about your friend Lily."

"Yes…"

"Have you heard from her lately?"

"No… she had to go up country due to a family bereavement."

"So, she told you where she was going?"

"No… I went to see her brother, to find out how she was. They… the men had told me she was poorly. So, I wanted to see how she was. But when I got there, I saw a note in the door saying closed due to a family bereavement."

"Closed!... what do you mean closed?" Hirst was intrigued.

"Oh... sorry I didn't say... Danny... Lily's brother runs a jeweller in Fowey and Lily lives with him."

"Ah... I see."

"Do you know if she was taken to hospital?"
"Sorry, no. I don't even know who the relative is. I didn't know they had relatives up country."

"What is Lilly's surname?" Hirst felt he should follow up on her.

"Oh, didn't I say... it's Lilly King."

They stayed a while to make sure the couple were settled and then said their goodbyes. After promising to let them know as soon as they had news on Lilly, they left. As they sat in the car, Hirst announced they were going to Fowey. On the journey they went over the details they had so far.

"I think we need to find the jewellers shop and chat to the local businesses around it. They may know how long the Kings were going to be away."

"Yes sir, I could go to a couple of them and ask around."

"So, we have a plan. But first we have to find the jewellers."

He parked up and glanced around the car park.

“Ah ha… that’s what we need.” He pointed towards a colourful notice board. It was a map of the town. They stood studying and after a short while found the street they needed. They walked in the town and headed towards the side street they required. Kings Jewellers was tucked down the bottom right of this narrow street.

“Here it is sir,” she pointed at a small shop and on the door, they saw the note. It was slightly scruffy and looked like it had been written in a rush. Hirst knocked the door a few times just in case. No answer.

“Well, it was worth a try.” He smiled.

“Right… I will go to the right, and you go to the left and see if anyone knows anything.”

“Yes sir.” Dixon turned and entered a small gift shop. The bell rang and a small woman came from the back out into the shop area.

“Good morning… I am PC Dixon. I was hoping you might be able to help us with a small enquiry,”

The woman looked interested and stepped forwards.

“I will try… what do you need to know?”

"You're next-door neighbour, Kings Jewellers. When did you last see them?

"Oh goodness... I'm not sure. Probably two weeks ago. They have gone to family a death I think."

"Did they say where they were going?"

"Oh no dear... I haven't spoken to Danny in a while. I only know they've gone because of the note on the door."

"Oh well, thank you for your help." Dixon turned to leave.

"Mind you... I was surprised he had not spoken to me before he went."

"Why?"

"Well... normally when either of us go away for a time we put out the bins for one another and take in the post."

"Do you have a key?"

"No... Danny normally gives me a key just before he leaves. But he didn't this time. But I suppose he forgot due to family commitments."

"I expect so." She turned and left and stepped out into the street again. The sun shone brightly, and it took her a moment to re-focus. She almost bumped into Hirst.

Embarrassed, she stepped back.

"Sorry Sir."

"No problem Dixon, any luck there?" he nodded towards the small gift shop.

"Well, it seems like they left in a hurry, as normally Danny would give the lady a key so she could pick up the post and put the bins out."

"I see... Well, I found out that as far as the proprietor of the small grocers knows, Lilly has not been poorly. He saw the couple about two weeks ago and they were both fine."

"Somethings not right about this sir."

"I agree." Hirst walked over to the door and tried it. Definitely locked.

"I wonder if there's a way to get to the back of the property." Dixon went back to the gift shop and called out.

"Hello... it's PC Dixon again." She waited for the woman to come back in the shop again.

"Hello.... Back again. Is there something else I can help you with?"

“Yes... is there a back entrance to the jewellers?”

“Yes dear, if you go back up the street, turn left and take another left, there is narrow road just used for deliveries.”

Thank you. You have been extremely helpful.” She turned back to Hirst and informed him. They walked back up the street and followed her directions.

“Here it is.” Hirst led the way. There was a high wooden fence with a small plaque naming the property. In the fencing was a large gate with a latch. They opened it and entered a small back yard. Apart from a couple of bins there was not much more. Apart from a small wooden bench with a large pot with flowers that would have looked grand if they had water. Hirst went to the door and after putting gloves on, he tried the door. This one was locked. They made sure the latch was shut well and left the property.

“Come on Dixon, we have some phone calls to make. First, we will try the local hospitals to see if Lilly is still in one and secondly, we should check if either have a criminal record as something smells about this whole story.”

Back in the station Dixon set to calling the hospitals while Hirst got his team to check through missing persons. When they checked through the criminal records, they could not find any link with Danny or Lilly King. They even checked to see if there were any road accidents involving two people… nothing.

"What we need if a photo of either." Hirst stated to his team.

"I want everyone to check papers, internet… anything you can think of. About ten minutes later, a knock-on Hirst door and a young PC entered.

"Yes… PC Toms, do you have something for me?"

"I think so sir… Kings Jewellers has a small website and there is a little picture near the bottom of the Danny King and his sister Lilly."

"Well done, Toms… good work."

They did their best to enhance the picture and sent it across the police network in the hope that someone may have seen the couple. But if not… they could keep an eye out for them.

TWENTY

Friday 25th June

"Detective John Hirst to see Detective David Taylor." The P C behind the counter stood up quickly and opened the side door to let him in.

P C Emma Dixon followed him through. They were shown to a small room off to the right. Before the P C left, she asked if they would like some coffee. They both accepted and she went to get some.

It was the following morning as that was when Detective David Taylor was available. They had to travel to the Cornwall and Devon police headquarters in St Austell and not the local station near Fowey.

The door opened and in came a P C with a tray with two cups of coffee and a small plate of biscuits. She was just placing them on the table when Detective Taylor walked in.

"Good… I see P C Wilder is looking after you."

Wilder turned slightly and acknowledged him and then left the room quickly.

John stood up and stretched out his hand and shook David's.

"It is good to see you, David."

"Same here, John and who do we have here?" He turned to look at Emma."

"This is P C Emma Dixon, a valued member of my team. I brought her along as she and I are working on a case together that might be of some interest to one of yours."

"Nice to meet you Dixon." Taylor shook her hand. He had a firm grip and his hands drowned hers almost like shaking a child's.

"Please sit." He gestured and sat opposite John.

To keep protocol The detectives called one another by their surnames as they were in the working confines, and they also had a lower rank person present.

"Well Hirst, bring me up to speed."

He started to relay the assault and robbery at Jake and Mary's to Taylor.

“What makes you think our cases overlap. Mine is a murder. I cannot see where our cases link.”

“Well, this is where it gets interesting. During our interview, Jake told us about a previous call to his place that unsettled him. A couple of men came to get information about a book that had been sold to Jake’s deceased friend James. This book should not have been so, as it belonged to the brother of a mutual friend.”

“What are you on about man?” Taylor started to get rattled. But Hirst was enjoying the tale and continued.

“I will get there… The so-called mutual friend was a Lilly King…” He stopped for a reaction.

“And…” His patience was wearing extremely thin now.

Hirst continued,

“Well… these two men according to Jake were no way friends of Lilly and they mentioned the book they wanted belonged to her brother Danny.”

“So, let me get this straight… you’ve come to me with a story of assault and robbery of a couple I know nothing about, and you think it is linked with my murder victim." Taylor was about to stand when Hirst opened his folder and produced a photo.

"Who are these people? Are they the couple Jake and Mary?" He stopped and looked closer and then the penny dropped.

"Christ… that's our Jane Doe… I'm sure it is." They had his interest now.

"Yes, I am sure your Jane Doe is Lilly King from Fowey. Hirst sat with pride and knew there was more. But he wanted Taylor to wait and drip feed him the information.

"We have more…" Hirst looked towards Dixon and said,

"I will let Dixon tell you the next part.

She took a deep breath and began.

"When I spoke to Mary and Jake, they told me of another visit that linked with the first from the two men. Not that Danny or Lily's names were mentioned but that of his friend James. You see the first visit was to get James address to regain this book of Danny's and the second visit, was from a woman… some story about returning belongings to James next of kin so his address was needed. But we feel it was to get to this book."

Taylor interrupted stating,

“That could be a coincidence and the request could be true.”

“Sorry Sir… but no… I checked at the hospital where this woman is supposed to work and they have not sent anyone as they had no need to, due to the fact they already had his address.”

“Okay… so we have a visit that mentions the name of my murder victim and the attempt to get an address where the deceased James lived.” He paused a moment, then added, “Then the second visit is a woman trying to get this same address.”

“Yes Sir… and now the attack and burglary with one of the items missing is Jakes address book.”

“And now someone has James address. Do we know where this James lived?” Taylor asked.

“Yes sir. There is a relative living there now.”

“We need to speak to them as soon as possible, they could be in danger, as these men do not sound as though they will stop until they get this book.”

“Yes Sir.” Hirst stepped in,

"We have had help from Detective Alan Thomas at Dorchester Station."

"Why Dorchester?"

"Because the address is in Dorset. And believe it or not, it was whilst they were there talking to the couple, it was suggested we try and speak to this Lilly about the book."

"I see... well, she can't help us now. "he pondered a moment then added,

"Do we know where her brother is?"

"No... all we know is they were going up country to a family bereavement."

"But surely he would be wondering where she is by now..."

"That's if he is alive... or maybe he killed her and is on the run." Hirst suggested they get a team down to the shop and check over the premisses.

Taylor arranged to meet with Hirst and work with him. Taylor wanted to bring his team up with the breakthrough so they could check records etc.

The two detectives stood outside Kings Jewellers. A team were brought in to gain access with the minimum damage.

They entered cautiously, not knowing what they would find. The shop area looked fine, nothing out of the ordinary. Out the back it looked a bit messy, but still nothing to get excited about. This could not be said about the flat above. The place had been ransacked. It look like an altercation had taken place. So, Taylor contacted his forensic team to get them in. Hirst would have liked to have had his team, but Taylor was extremely forceful in getting his way. Even Hirst knew what Taylor was like. It was pointless arguing.

Jerry turned up with his team and was notably pleasant to Hirst and markedly unpleasant to Taylor. He could not resist. As the team worked in the flat upstairs, Jerry stated

"Someone was looking for something."

"The thing is... did he find it?" Taylor queried.

"He... it could have been a female." Hirst added.

"No... I doubt it." Jerry stated.

"Why?" Taylor wanted to put Jerry on the spot.

“Because… I have examined the body and by the marks and force on her neck it took strength or extreme rage.”

“Well, let’s hope we can get some fingerprints that will help.”

At Meadow View the security firm worked on the security system. It was surprisingly quick. As the outside had been completed. So, it was just setting up the interior system and instructing Andy and Becky on how to set up. When the firm left Andy and Becky felt a lot happier. They hoped they would never have to use it. Around eleven the phone rang; Becky went to answer.

“Hello…”

There was silence at the other end. So, Becky repeated,

“Hello…”

A man’s voice spoke,

“Do I have the right number for Andy Randell?”

“Um… yes. Shall I get him for you?”

“Yes please.”

“Who shall I say is calling?”

"Oh, just say a friend. He will recognise my voice. I want it to be a surprise."

She stopped for a moment, then replied, "Okay, I won't be a moment."

Andy was out in the back garden trying to get the weeds under control when Becky called. "Andy a friend is on the phone."

"Who?"

"I don't know, he said you would recognise his voice." As Andy stepped in the kitchen and quickly wiped his hands. He thought who did I give this number to?

He entered the living room and picked up the phone.

"Hello…"

"Is that Andy?" came the answer.

Andy sounded guarded as he replied

"Yes…"

"Andy… you don't know me. But I know you from your friend Jake." Andy went white as a sheet. Who the hell was he!!

"Who are you? What do you want?"

"You don't need to know who I am. All you need to do is return my property."

He sounded cold and menacing.

“Your property! What property?”

“My book and its contents.” He hissed.

“Book?” Becky’s interest was sparked now, and she looked concerned as Andy looked as if all the colours had drain from his face.

“I don’t know what you mean. What’s this book called and what do you mean by its contents?” Andy tried as hard as he could to keep calm and in control.

“Stolen. And you know its contents, **my bloody blue diamond.”** He had raised his voice now and you could almost imagine the heat coming down the phone lines to burn him.

“Diamond…” Andy spoke in slow motion, almost in a whisper.

“I have not got your diamond. The book was empty, honestly.”

“**Don’t lie to me.”** He shouted.

“I’m not, the book was empty.” Andy was starting to panic now. What could he say to convince him?

“Listen lad… it won’t be just a broken pane of glass if you don’t give back my diamond.”

“How can I give you something I’ve never had or even seen?” Andy did not like where this conversation was going.

“Where’s the book? It wasn’t in the house?”

“We don’t have it anymore.”

“What do you mean?

“The police have it.”

“WHAT!!” Jimmy looked like he would burst a blood vessel. The line went silent for a moment while Jimmy thought. He then continued.

“Why would the police want the book if my diamond wasn’t in it?”

“They said for fingerprints. They were looking for fingerprints.”

Jimmy sighed as he knew his would not be on it. He knew he had hit a brick wall.

“I will be watching you and your partner. So, when you find my diamond expect a visit.” With that he slammed the phone down.

Andy just sat with the receiver in his hand, speechless almost frozen to the spot.

“Andy… love … what is it?” she had never seen him like this before and it frightened her. He re placed the receiver down slowly and as calmly as possible told Becky of the conversation.

" Andy. We have to call the police right now."

"I know… we cannot take any chances." He picked up the phone again and also used the card Detective Thomas had given him. His hands were shaking as he dialled. The number put him straight through to Thomas office. He picked up the phone and was surprised to hear from Andy so soon.

"Detective Thomas… we have had a phone call that I think was our attempted burglar."

"Can you tell me what he said?" Thomas grabbed a pad and pen. He moved to the door with his phone in his hand and beckoned Collins over. She entered and sat down. Thomas quickly put the phone on speaker and they both listened to Andy repeat as much as he could remember.

"Well, Andy I am glad you called. Stay where you are, and I will be along as soon as possible. Do not open the door to anyone apart from me… okay."

"Yes sir." Andy replaced the phone and went to lock both doors and wait.

Meanwhile, Thomas grabbed his coat and closely followed by Collins they left the station.

Within fifteen minutes, they arrived at Meadow View. Thomas and Collins walked up to the door and rang the bell.

"Who is it?" Andy called.

"It's Detective Thomas and Sergeant Collins Andy." He pushed a card through the letterbox so Andy could be assured it was them. Moments later they were all sat in the kitchen around the table with a hot drink.

"Well, Andy it looks like this man that called you and threatened you, has admitted he was the one that entered your house."

"True."

"We also know what was in your book." Thomas looked at Andy waiting to see how he would respond. It was Becky that answered.

"There wasn't anything in the book when I found it. Certainly not a diamond." She felt her heart thumping in her chest with worry. Did they think she and Andy had hidden it? Surely not.

Collins calmy asked,

"Becky… have you checked the small room just in case the diamond had fallen out of the book before you found it?"

"Well, no… of course not. We only found out what was meant to be in the book today through that awful phone call." She glanced at Andy quizzically.

"Would you mind if you and I took a look?"

"No… "she stood up and Collins followed her up to the small room.

Collins gave the room a scan briefly, then she asked,

"Becky… I know you have sorted these books… but can we check them all? It's just in case something is tucked behind one."

"That's fine by me. I want to find it."

So, they both set to removing the books and replacing once checked. Afterwards they checked the rest of the room thoroughly with no avail. When they entered the kitchen again, Andy and Thomas were finishing up details on the next move planned. Andy had agreed to have his phone tapped for a while and Thomas had assured that there would be a police presence at all times to ensure their safety. This helped the couple relax a bit. They promised not to venture out alone. But always be together.

TWENTY-ONE

Saturday 26th June

Hirst was sat in his office when the call came in from Thomas. He informed them about the phone call to Andy and they both agreed that the possibilities were extremely high that the prints at Meadow View were of one of the two men that had visited Jake several days ago as they were determined to get the address. As soon as Hirst received the prints, he would check through the records to see if they match any other misdemeanours, especially in the area.

Later that day Hirst was interrupted by a tap on his door.

“Come...” he looked up from his desk, waiting to see who had disturbed his work.”

PC Emma Dixon entered and apologised for the interruption.

“No need… do you have anything we can use?”

“I am not sure sir… There is a match between the print at Meadow View and wait for it… one from Kings Jewellers.” She stood smiling and waiting for his reaction.

“Oh my god… our killer maybe in Dorset.”

“Yes sir.”

“I need to get Detective Taylor right away. Once again, he caught hold of the phone and rang him.

“Hello John… have you got something for us?”

“I reckon we have Dave. You know you found fingerprints in King’s jewellers… Well, one of your prints match the prints of a burglary down in Dorset.”

“That was a lucky break. Was it another jeweller?”

“No… it was at Meadow View. And we have more… the couple that live there, have been threatened by this person.”

“Christ…”

John continued to explain the details and they agreed that it had to be one of the men that had visited Jake. Not necessarily the two that had ransacked his home.

“We have to visit the elderly couple and try and get a description of the men.” Taylor felt sure they were closing in on them.

“Yes… and I think we should also have a composite artist with us.”

Taylor agreed and Hirst made a call to Jake to arrange a visit later in the day.

Back in Weymouth, Jimmy and Ken were sat in his range rover trying to work out their next step.

“I’m sure that little twerp is lying. I think he has my diamond and has decided to keep it for his self.”

Ken was not so sure, when he had listened in on the conversation between Jimmy and Andy, he was sure Andy was telling the truth… but when Jimmy had a bee in his bonnet, there was no going back.

"Jimmy… I think we need to keep our heads down. I mean the police are all over that couple, so how can we get to them?"

"We need to find a good viewing spot, so we can keep a close eye on them."

"Yeah, but where?"

Hirst drove Taylor and the sketch artist, Julie, to Jake and Marys home. As they pulled up and parked, Hirst switched off the engine and turned to Taylor.

"Taylor… Jake is pretty switched on, but Mary is very fragile at the moment."

"Okay… if you want you can lead the questions and I will add any ones I need."

John nodded and they with Julie, got out of the car. Jake had heard the car pull up and recognised the driver. So, he had the door open as they approached.

"Hello Detective Hirst, I hope you have some good news for us."

"I'm afraid not yet Jake. This is my colleague Detective Taylor and Julie. She is a sketch artist here to help us. Would it be convenient to come in and ask a few more questions please?"

"Of course... do come in. Mary is in the living room resting. She will be pleased to see you. Mind you it's a shame P C Dixon isn't with you... Marys took a liking to her. She is such a lovely friendly lady." They entered the living room to find Mary sat in an armchair knitting. As soon as she saw the visitors, she started to rise.

"Please stay where you are Mary, there's no need to get up." Hirst smiled as he spoke and added,

"How are you today?"

"Oh... I've been better, but I cannot complain. Just a bit jumpy, but that will go soon I hope."

"I'm sure it will. But give it time Mary... you went through an awful ordeal."

She smiled at him, then turned towards Taylor as if to say who are you.

"Oh, please forgive my manners Mary." He introduced Taylor and Julie and they all sat down. After the proper introductions, Hirst began.

“Jake… when you had the first visit of the two men asking about a book of Danny’s can you give us as much detail you can remember?”

“I will try. There were two men, as I said before. The main one that spoke… he were tall. About six feet. I remember he had dark eyes. Mind you I’m not sure what colour. But they were dark… almost menacing if you get my drift.”

“Good Jake… you’re doing well. Continue please.” Hirst encouraged.

“Well… he came across quite friendly at first. But then when I told him James had died, he shouted crap… then seconds later he apologised. I thought it were a bit strange behaviour. Then came the questions where he lived, was there anyone living there. He also asked if I had his address. I’m afraid I lied, but now it would have been true. Mind you Andy has given me his number and I will get his address from him soon.

“Andy!” Taylor asked.

“Yes, Andy and Becky, they live in James home now. Oh, the poor things had a break in Tuesday night. I don’t know what the world is coming to, I really don’t.”

"Oh yes, you mean Andrew and Becky. Yes, we heard. It is very upsetting." Hirst shot a glance at Taylor, then he asked Jake to try and describe the second man.

"He was a quiet man; I mean he didn't say a lot. But he was a man that you wouldn't argue with to be sure. He were tall and had muscles in his arms like Popeye."

"Is there anything else you can tell us about this second man? Like his hair colour or eyes."

"To be honest... no. Only what hair he had was like bristle. It were his size that I focused on... Sorry."

"No worries Jake, if you wouldn't mind, I'm going to ask you to sit with Julie and go over any details you do remember with her. She will attempt to draw them and let's see if we can get a likeness." Hirst smiled at Julie and Jake moved into the kitchen and sat to the small table to start.

Meanwhile Hirst and Taylor went across the road to talk to Janet and Clive.

Janet had been stood looking out of her kitchen window observing the coming and goings at Jake and Marys. As soon as she realised the detectives were heading her way, she shot back away from the window and tried to keep calm and act surprised when they rang the doorbell.

As soon as she had the door open, she gushed

“Oh Detective… Hirst, isn’t it?”

“Yes, Janet how good of you to remember.” He stretched out a hand and greeted her. She smiled, then turned to Taylor.

“Oh, sorry Janet… this is my colleague Detective Taylor.” He nodded curtly.

She invited them in, and they sat down in the living room. Janet could not wait to get started. She felt excited and keen to be involved.

“I am afraid my husband is out, but how can I help you? Detectives!” she smiled at both.

It was Hirst that answered because he could see that Taylor took an instant dislike to Janet.

“Janet we were hoping you could think back to about a week before Jake and Marys unfortunate experience.”

“Right?”

“Did you observe any strangers turn up at their place at all?”

"Um… no I'm afraid not."

"Are you sure? Think…" Taylor almost sounded irritated. Hirst shot him a disapproval look.

"I said no… I don't stand watching my neighbours all day long."

Hirst jumped in quickly.

"Of course not, we are grateful for all your help. We won't take up anymore of your time Jackie." He stood up and stretched out his hand to her. She took it gratefully and just nodded a goodbye to Taylor.

Back in the drive as they left her home, Hirst turned on Taylor.

"Look man…there was no need to be so rude to her."

"Well, she is nothing but a nosey busy body."

"That might be true. But she could have been extremely helpful to our investigation."

They walked back to Jake and Marys in silence. There were times Taylor got on Hirst nerves, and this was one. He seemed to be more arrogant as he got closer to retirement.

Mary answered the door and let them in as Julie was just finishing up.

Hirst looked at Julie and she nodded.

“You have done well. We will leave you now to the rest of your day. If you think of anything else, please call us and if you are worried about anything that does not feel right call… Okay?”

“Yes, Detective Hirst we will.”

The two detectives stood up and shook hands with Jake and Mary and once again thanked them for their help.

Back in the car, Hirst turned to Julie,

“Well, how do you think it went?”

“Not too bad, I feel Jake remembered more on one than the other.” She passed the sketches to Hirst.

“Hmmm I see what you mean.” He pointed to one of the men.

“This one looks like a nasty piece of work and the other… well… cannot be sure what to think, as the only thing is… he is almost bald, and he is the one Jake said was muscular.”

“It’s a start.” Taylor added.

TWENTY-TWO

Saturday 26th pm

Jimmy spent the whole morning spoiling Sandy with small gifts of perfume. He would have bought her a piece of jewellery, but he was in no mood to enter a jeweller. There was an alternate reason. Jimmy intended to be away for possibly a couple days.

“Why do you have to stay away?” Sandy grumbled.

“Babes… I told you. This job needs Ken and I to protect some awfully expensive tools especially overnight. It should only be a couple of days.”

“But why you? Can’t Ken do it on his own?”

“No love… look the money is extremely good for this part of the job and you know that will mean, a beautiful gift for my beautiful girl.” He cupped her chin in his hand and bent and kissed her tenderly on the lips. She melted as he looked deep in her eyes and winked playfully at her. She could not resist Jimmy. As a new wife she wanted to please him. In the hotel there were leaflets of local places to visit. Amongst them a pamphlet about The Retreat, a pamper weekend. Jimmy called them to see if Sandy could come over at short notice. They agreed especially after he enticed them with extra cash.

After Sandy had packed a small bag, Jimmy took it to the car. He arranged with the hotel to keep the rooms on even though they would not be there. He hoped a couple of days would be enough. His plan was to drop Sandy off at The Retreat near Wareham, then they would get their supplies needed to keep them going.

So, now it was Saturday afternoon. Jimmy and Ken had just dropped Sandy off and after a long goodbye between Sandy and Jimmy they were on their way.

"Right now, to business." Jimmy stated.

"The supermarket?" Ken asked.

"Yeah… the supermarket, we need some food and also a pair of binoculars."

"What? Why do we need binoculars?"

"You'll see…" he smiled then continued,

"I need a good pair of night vision ones."

"Where the hell are we going to get them?"

Jimmy pulled in a lay by and took out his phone. He went on the internet and put in a search. He noticed Argos sold them, so. He put in a search to find the closest branch he could pick a pair up. He struck lucky as they had a pair available in Wareham. In Wareham they picked up the binoculars and enough food to keep them going a while. They drove out towards a little place called Lower Waterston and parked in a lay by near Waterston Manor.

"Come on." Jimmy reached for the door handle and stepped out of the Range Rover. He went to the boot and took out the binoculars.

"Where are we going? We can't just go up to the house in broad daylight." Ken looked worried as if to say Jimmy had gone mad.

"Corse not." He smirked,

"Anyway, we are nowhere near Meadow View."

"So, what are we doing?"

"You'll see." He started to walk up the road in the direction of Druce.

"Christ Jimmy we are a long way from the house."

"I know, but bear with me."

They walked on up a small incline and up to their left were a few farm cottages sat along the edge of the narrow road. A pair of semi-detached rendered properties. As the continued on further another pair of semi-detached properties, these were set back a bit and were red brick. They backed onto meadows with beautiful views. Moving on they came to some old brick rendered barns. Jimmy stopped for a moment to check them out. But he soon moved on, as he saw they were definitely in use. Farm animals were inside, and he saw a young farmer attending the young lambs. Jimmy was keen not to draw attention to themselves. The area opened up to their left with hedging to the right. As the road was narrow, they had to stop walking and step up into the hedging slightly as a car came by. At one time when they stood waiting for a car to past, Jimmy looked out over the road, out over the fields. He caught sight of what he had been looking for and as the car passed Ken stepped back down whilst

Jimmy stayed put and raised the binoculars to his eyes.

"Yes… just what I thought." He mumbled to himself. "Now how can we get there?" he contemplated.

"What are you on about?" Ken asked.

Jimmy stepped down back into the road and as he spoke, he crossed the road to the left alongside a low hedge.

"Without making it obvious, look across the field to your left."

"Yeah, what am I supposed to see?" he queried.

"A small hut."

"Where?" Ken could not see it.

"It's out across the second field." He pointed quickly.

"Oh yeah… hey why have I got to be careful not to point it out when you can?"

"Because I have the binoculars and if anyone saw me, they would think I am bird watching."

"Oh." Ken still could not work it out but decided not to argue. They ambled along slowly looking as they went for a gap in the hedge or better still a small gate. They had to settle for a gap. Ken was about to step through, Jimmy stopped him.

"What are you doing?" he hissed.

"I thought you wanted to go to the hut."

"Not now man. In broad daylight, you just as well put a big sign out saying we're here."

"Sorry mate, I wasn't thinking."

"No, you were not. We need to be able to find this gap later tonight." Jimmy fumbled in his pockets to find something that he might see in the dark. All he had was some loose change, his car keys, and a hanky.

"This will do." He opened his hanky out and rolled it to make it as long as possible and quickly tied it to a twig just inside the hedging in the gap. He took another look out into the fields and noted the route they would venture later. Then he turned back the way they had come.

"Come on, let's get a takeaway." Ken liked the sound of that and with a spring in his step he followed Jimmy back to the car.

Meanwhile at Meadow View Andy and Becky were sat in their living room wondering what to do. They did not want to go anywhere.

“You know what we should do,” Andy suddenly announced.

“What?”

“Try and workout where James hid this diamond.”

“We have cleaned everything, so it’s not in the house. That only leaves outside.”

“Yes possibly, unless he took it somewhere else.”

“Well, if he did… we will never know.” She looked at Andy glumly. He took her in his arms,

“I’m sorry Becky.”

“What do you mean?” she pulled away from him and looked at him curiously.

“Bringing you into this mess.”

She smiled at him

“Don’t be silly Andy. For one thing it’s not your fault all of this. And another thing I will be with you all the way until this is sorted.”

“And after that?” he asked.

“I’m not going anywhere you daft ninny. “she hugged him firmly.

Back in Saltash Police Station the team working with Hirst were gathered for a briefing.

“Right, everyone I need your attention…” he hesitated a moment to ensure they were listening.

“Okay… we have a composite picture of two men of interest. He passed copies around so they could all have a good look. A hand shot up. It was Dixon,

“Sir do we know anything about these men? Like where they come from.”

“I’m afraid not… All we have on them is… They are supposably local but not confirmed. They work together and one of them… not sure which one has left his fingerprints at Kings Jewellery shop and also at Meadow View in Druce Dorset.”

“Not a lot to go on Sir.”

"I know, but thanks to Jake we have some kind of picture to go by for likeness." Hirst stopped and turned to Taylor.

"This is Detective Taylor and Sergeant Wheely of Cornwall and Devon police headquarters in Austell, he would like a few words."

"Thank you, Hirst." He cleared his throat for attention.

"Right as you are all aware I am leading a murder case of an elderly woman, now identified as a Miss Lilly King. She is the sister of Mr. Daniel King, the proprietor of Kings Jeweller in Fowey. We are still looking for Daniel. He seems to have disappeared. We are led to believe he has gone up country for a family bereavement."

PC Carter put his hand up to ask a question.

"Yes..." came an abrupt response from Taylor to which Carter almost sank back in his chair regretting putting his hand up.

"Um... Sir..."

"Spit it out man." Barked Taylor.

It was Hirsts turn to clear his throat loudly and it worked.

“Sorry lad. what’s your name?” Taylor asked in a better voice.

“Carter Sir.”

“Well, Carter, continue.”

“I was only going to ask, who told us Daniel had gone up country?”

“Good question lad.” He hesitated to get them back on side, realising how abrupt he had been, he smiled. It did not suit his face, he looked more like he had chewed a wasp. “Maybe Hirst can tell you.” He turned towards him and nodded.

“PC Carter, it was our friend Jake. He was told by these two men in the pictures. So unfortunately, it may be a lie… But then we saw a note on the door of Kings Jeweller stating the same.” Carter nodded and Hirst turned back to Taylor.

“PC Carter was at the scene when we first met Jake and Mary. He took a statement from your friend Janet Watts.” Hirst could not resist putting in that little comment, to which gave the response, as if he had swallowed the wasp alive.

Clearing his throat for the second time, Taylor pulled a picture from his folder and held it up.

"Right, I need your help with tracking down this man." He pointed at the picture of Danny King.

"You have a picture of him?" he questioned.

"Yes, they do, it was PC Toms that found it."

Yet another dig, he was determined his team would get recognition for their work on this case. Sergeant Wheely interrupted,

"Sir why are we searching for Lilly's brother? Surely he wouldn't have killed her!"

"We cannot rule him out and besides that, we need to know what happened in his flat and where he is."

"True Sir." Wheely stepped back and waited for Taylor to continue.

"Okay... what we know is Lilly King was strangled in the flat above Kings Jewellers and before you ask how... I will explain. Lily was found on the beach near Trebarwith on Sunday 20th June. She was only wearing a bathrobe. Her feet were bare and there were no marks on the soles of her feet to say she had a struggle on the beach with whoever killed her. "he paused a moment, then continued. "Now back at the Jeweller, in the flat above there were signs of a struggle and some kind of search. Downstairs in the shop area there is only a handwritten sign on the door." He picked up a photocopy of the sign "Closed due to bereavement".

Hirst asked,

"Do we know if anything was stolen from the jewellers yet."

"No, not yet our team are going through his records as we speak. But Jerry our in forensics did find a spot of blood in the small back room down on the corner of some shelving. We do not know whose blood it is. All we know it is not Lilly's."

Dixon raised her hand asking,

"Sir do we think Daniel had a falling out with his sister? Killed her, then drove her to this beach and left her there."

"That is a possibility… we have not found his car or him as yet. What we need to do, is send these pictures to Detective Thomas at Dorchester. He can then keep an eye open for them especially near Meadow View."

Sergeant Peggy Colins tapped on Thomas's office door.

"Enter."

"Gov… we have some composite pictures come through from Detective Hirst of the two men that maybe in our area."

"Oh, good let's have a look." He stretched out his hand to take them from her.

"I do not think our young couple will want to tackle these men." He said as he looked at them,

"I know what you mean. Do we have any more information on them?"

"No, not yet. Peggy… do we have a team at their home?

"Yes Gov…they are placed in close proximity of the house, keeping a watch on any comings or goings."

"That's good. You finish up now and get home. Get some rest, I think we have another busy day ahead."

"Yes Gov… see you in the morning." She turned and left.

Alan sat in his office mulling over details. He had a feeling they were missing something, but he could not think what. Maybe he should do the same and go home get some sleep and start with a fresh head in the morning.

Around nine in the evening Jimmy pulled into a lay by not far from Meadow View. It was the one Andy had met George Willis on the day they went to view. Jimmy quickly turned his lights off.

"Ken... open that gate quickly." He whispered.

"Okay." Ken jumped out and set to opening it. Jimmy didn't know why he whispered but still he acted as cautious as possible as he gently pulled off the roadside and drove his Range Rover into a field alongside hedging, enough to be sure it could not be seen from the road. The pair took a rucksack each and placed them on their backs and left the field ensuring the gate was closed as before and headed up the road away from Meadow View. They intended to get back to the gap in the hedging where they earlier left Jimmy's hanky. It took them about twenty minutes to get there. Then they had to make their way through the hedging and out into the first field. They walked rapidly towards the hedgerow on their left and followed it down towards a corner. Once there, they had to search for a small pathway that led through to the next field. Eventually they found it and aimed for the hut. They only had a couple of barb wire strands to contend with. As quickly as possible they entered the hut. The darkness swallowed them and enveloped them like thick dark curtains. Once their eyes accustomed to the blackness they saw inside the small shelter, a table and chair. They took their rucksacks off and placed them on the table. Jimmy caught hold of his binoculars and told Ken he would be back shortly. He left the hut and moved carefully away towards the house in the distance.

TWENTY-THREE

Sunday 27th

Alan Thomas was sat in his office early, especially for a Sunday. He had not slept so well, he kept thinking what he was missing, he always followed his own intuition. So, he had to work out what. When Peggy arrived, he called her into the office.

"Listen, Peggy, you know when I get a feeling, I've missed something..."

"Yes..."

"Well, I need you to help me work out what it is."

So, for the next hour they sat and went through everything they knew about the whole case. Peggy decided to get a coffee for them both.

"Hopefully, it will wake up my brain." She laughed as she left the room. Alan sat with all the details in front of him. He started to talk to himself.

"These two men arrive at Jakes and tell a story about his friend Lilly, and then she turns up dead."

"You know it's the first sign of madness?" Peggy walked in with the coffees.

"Thank you, Collins." He grunted, then laughed.

"So Gov... what were you saying?"

"The two men turn up at Jakes and tell a story about Lilly and she turns up dead. So, let's break it down.

"Gov...!" she looked at him confused.

“First... the two men turn up at Jakes. Question, how did they know his address and how did they get there?”

“Well, I don’t know how they knew his address, but... they drove there.”

“Do we have details on the car?” He shuffled his paperwork.

“No.”

Alan picked up his phone and called Hirst.

“John... Alan Thomas,”

“Hello Alan, is our couple safe?”

“As far as I know, we have a team keeping a close eye on them. What I’m ringing about is... Do you know what car these men were driving when they visited Jake and Mary?”

“To be honest Alan I don’t know. But leave it with me and I will get back to you.”

“Thanks John.”

In Saltash Police Station Hirst called Jake. “Hello Jake, I hope you and Mary are well. I’m sorry to call so early”.

“Detective Hirst, yes we are fine each day getting better.” He sounded very cheerful.

“Good, good… I wonder if you happened to notice the car that the two men drove, the day they visited you.” Hirst sat with anticipation.

“Um… I know it was one of those big cars. You know those four be fours… Sorry I can’t tell you the make or model. “

“Don’t worry Jake, that is very helpful, I don’t suppose you know what colour it was.”

“It was a dark colour… I think it was black… no it might have been dark blue.”

“That’s fine Jake you have done well. Thank you.”

Hirst was about to put the phone down when Jake added,

“Oh, it had a personalized number plate.”

Hirst had a rush of optimism,

“Can you remember it?”

“Sorry… no… there might have been a J in the plate number. I thought at the time my initial.”

“Well done, Jake, thank you again.”

Hirst could not wait to inform the others of this information.

Back in Austell headquarters, Taylor was in full swing. He had sent Wheely out to Fowey to get as much detail on Danny and Lily as possible. When Wheely questioned that it was a Sunday, Taylor roared back.

"Good... that means the neighbours will be in."

Wheely felt stupid and left for Fowey as quickly as possible.

He reached the jewellers around ten and spoke with the two PC's stood keeping an eye on the premises.

"Any sign of our man returning?

"No, Sergeant, it's all quiet here."

"Ok, carry on." He nodded and went to a side door of the small gift shop next door. He rang the bell and waited. He could hear from behind the door someone thumping down the stairs muttering

“It better not be those youngster’s messing with my bell again.” As Wheely could hear her well, he called out…

“Sorry to call on you on a Sunday… It’s the police. Can I have a few words.”

The woman from behind the door opened it and rather flushed answered.

“Sorry young man. I thought it was the young ones messing again.”

Wheely stood holding his card up for her to see.

“Yes. Do you want to come in.”? He agreed and followed her up the stairs to a small flat above the shop.

“I am about to have a cup of coffee; would you like to join me?”

“That’s extremely kind of you. I am Sergeant Wheely from Austell police station.”

“Nice to meet you Sergeant… I am Joan Gould, I own and run the gift shop downstairs. How can I help you?

She brought two mugs of coffee through to the small sitting room and asked if he took milk or sugar.

"Both please, just one sugar thank you." Wheely took a sip and smiled.

"That's good coffee, thank you."

She smiled gratefully and sat back in her chair.

"I gather you know why we; the police are around at the moment."

"Yes... poor Lilly." She looked slightly upset and then cleared her throat.

"Could you please tell me what you know about Danny and Lilly? Like, how well did they get on."

"Get on!! Goodness me.... Danny and Lilly were devoted to each other. They were never apart. She looked after him well. I mean you only had to look at him." She smiled.

"What do you mean? Look at him."

"Oh, I'm being cheeky. He was rather overweight. I think it was all the cakes Lilly fed him. Mind you I can't talk." She laughed.

"So, there was no animosity between them?"

"No... no dear none. They even went out on a Sunday together for picnics."

“Did either of them drive?”

“Yes dear, they both drove. They shared the car. He would use it sometimes to get stock and she would take it to either go to the sales or visit friends.”

“Do you know any of her friends?”

“Not personally… but I have met Jake and Mary briefly, I don’t know their surname.”

“No need… we know them thank you.”

“Jake came over about a week ago or more looking for Lilly, until he saw the note. I saw him looking. I could not go out and speak to him as I had a customer in the shop at the time.”

“One last question, if you don’t mind. Do you know what car Danny drives?”

“Um, yes it’s an old Austin Allegro. He’s had it for years.”

“Do you know how old it is? Or the colour.”

“I don’t know the age sorry… but I can tell you it’s red.”

“Thank you. You have been extremely helpful Joan.” Wheely stood up and stretched out his hand to thank her. As they walked down the stairs, Joan added,

“I hope you find Danny soon. Poor man doesn’t know about Lilly. He will be devastated.”

“We plan to find him soon… thank you again. goodbye.”

Back out in the street, Wheely stood for a short time just looking around. It was peaceful, hardly anyone about.

Just a young couple walking hand in hand down towards him. They took one look towards the jeweller and stopped. The young man turned to his girlfriend and said,

“It looks like we will have to look in other jewellers for that ring.”

She in return, squeezed his hand and they turned on the spot and left.

Wheely went to one of the PC’s again,

“Do you have the keys for the jewellers with you?”

“Yes Sergeant.” He fished in his pocket and held them out for Wheely.

“I am going into the back to look for something in the filing cabinet. Can you join me?”

“Yes Sergeant.”

Due to the nature of the contents of the shop, Wheely needed a witness to ensure he would, or could not be accused of stealing anything.

He unlocked and they entered… locking the door behind them. It felt cold and dark, you could almost feel or taste the death of Lilly in the place. They made their way back into the ridiculously small room where a four-drawer metal filing cabinet stood. It had seen better days, several small dents and a bit of rust showing through the light grey colour. Strangely, the keys were in the top drawer. Wheely noted that if he; Danny, was about to travel up country for a while, surely, he would have locked his filing cabinet. Still, it did mean that Wheely could look in the drawers for details on the car, hopefully…

He pulled out the top drawer and was pleasantly surprised to see all folders neatly labelled. This made his search a lot easier. He found the appropriate folder and lifted it out.

He went to his pocket and pulled out a large clear plastic bag with a zip top. Gently he placed the whole folder and its contents into the bag and sealed it. He wrote on the bag details of time and date and both officers signed.

Meanwhile at Meadow View, to be precise, in the small hut, Jimmy and Ken had had a cold uncomfortable night.

"I need a pee, Jimmy... I can't do it here."

"Christ Ken... look if you have to go out. Don't open the door too much and keep really low and get round the back. But be quick. We don't want anyone to see us." Jimmy whispered and Ken just nodded and went for the door.

"Wait a minute I will check there's no-one around." He took his binoculars and put them up to a small hole and could just see enough of the area back down the pathway towards the house.

"All clear but be quick."

Ken moved as quickly as he could. He was stiff from the uncomfortable position he had slept. Which was not a lot. As he closed the door, Jimmy decided to have a pee in the corner of the shed while he was alone. Moments later Ken opened the door slightly and squeezed back in.

He sniffed,

“Christ, I didn’t pee on my trousers, did I?” He looked down and could not see anything. Jimmy just smirked and kept silent.

Ken whispered…

"What can you see from here?”

“A small bit… but to be honest not as much as I hoped for. I can just about see the back door of the house and towards the barn. I reckon we will have to find somewhere better. But we will have to stay here till dark before we move.”

“Christ, Jimmy. What do we do? Play I bloody spy.” Jimmy chuckled.

“Yeah Ken. I spy with my little eye something beginning with p.”

“What!” Jimmy was in no mood to play silly buggers.

“I spy with my little eye something beginning with p.” he repeated.

“What?”

“Your prick… silly bugger, do your flies up.”

Ken quickly looked down and pulled up his zip.

“That’s because I was in a hurry to get back in the hut.”

Ken’s stomach rumbled, he was hungry, so they both went to their bags and pulled out some sandwiches and they had a can of costa coffee each.

“This tastes bloody awful. I prefer a hot coffee.” Jimmy stated to which Ken agreed, but they still ate and drank as it would be a long day ahead.

“We have to think of a better plan Ken, so get your brain into gear. We need something sorted by the time we leave here tonight, or that’s a whole day wasted.”

“True.” Ken looked glum and just sat on the floor contemplating.

In Meadow View, Andy and Becky had just finished eating their lunch and were stood in the kitchen washing up the plates. Andy looked miles away thinking.

Becky turned and saw him.

“What is it?”

“I don’t know, there has to be clues somewhere for us to follow and find the diamond. It said so in his journal.”

“True… but you have read it.”

“I know. So, I must be missing something.”

“To be honest Andy if we find it, I would be tempted to give it to this man that rang you, to get him away from us.”

“Sweetie… we can’t.”

“Why?”

“For one thing we don’t know how to contact him. And another thing he has probably killed Jakes friend Lilly.”

“You don’t know that.”

“No… true… but I just don’t trust him, whoever he is.”

After they had packed away the dishes, they gathered the journal and diary and went into the living room and sat together to look again at James’s writings.

They turned to the page with the title ‘Clues’.

Andy read it aloud again.

“Where did it come from…? Who do I trust?

Note… for whoever has my journal.

If you have found 'Stolen' and you are my heir. Then you have started the journey.

But if you are not…then it will be lost for ever."

"It still makes no sense." Becky stated.

"Okay… we have to think… what could we do that someone else couldn't?"

"I don't know." She looked at him as puzzled as ever.

"Well, I am his heir… and he put in clauses."

"Yeah!"

"Let's go through them, maybe one will trigger something."

"Okay… one, you had to sign in trust."

"Well, that's nothing to do with the property and it's belongings."

No-one could access his bank account apart from you."

"True… but I doubt the diamond is at the bank."

"It could be." She mused.

"Well, I suppose we ought to look. I will call the bank and arrange a meeting with them as soon as possible."

"We can't do anything until Monday morning. Okay, So, what else did you have control on." She asked.

"There was the strange thing about no-one entering the house without me."

"Yeah, that was a weird thing." She agreed.

"So, is it in the house?"

TWENTY-FOUR

Monday 28th

Wheely set to work getting all the information on Danny's Allegro. He had the registration and colour. So, he presented it to Taylor. "Good work Wheely. Now we need to send it to all stations on the network to keep an eye open for it."

"Yes Sir." Wheely stood expecting more from Taylor.

"Well, get on with it man."

"Yes Sir." Wheely left him quickly muttering under his breath,

"Miserable old sod."

Taylor picked up the phone and called Hirst at Saltash.

"John... it's Taylor... we have a car that may be of interest. An Allegro. It belongs to Daniel King. The details are coming your way." He sounded smug as he spoke.

"It's funny you should call me about a car... as I have one for you to keep a look out for also." He gave the details of the possible four be four that had a personalised number plate.

"Have the couple had any more contact with this unknown burglar?" Taylor asked.

"No. nothing yet and my men have been closely keeping an eye on them. Say Dave... if this man is more than a burglar... he may be the murderer... he could be driving the Allegro of Danny's."

“But if that’s true where is Danny and how would Danny be able to go up country for the family?”

Questions kept flying back and forth like a game of tennis. And if this were so… then Taylor would say advantage Taylor.

Jimmy woke slightly later than he wanted. But by the time he and Ken got back to the car and travelled back to Weymouth, it was rather late. The proprietor of the hotel was not too happy been woken up in the early hours. But he knew not to complain, he had been warned by Davey what Jimmy could be like. It was only because he owed a favour to Davey, he had said yes to having such a man stay. After a long soak in the bath Jimmy’s head hit the pillow and he was sound asleep.

Ken was already eating his large breakfast when Jimmy walked into the dining room. The waitress came across with hot coffee and asked what he would like for breakfast.

“I think I will have the same as my friend please love and for seconds, you.” He winked and she blushed hurrying away.

“Jimmy man you’ve only been married a few weeks.”

"And... you know I need more than one woman to keep me happy and anyway the misses isn't here."

Ken looked at him slightly surprised, to which Jimmy suddenly laughed.

"Hey Ken... got you going there."

The waitress delivered his plate of food gingerly and left the confines of the table as quickly as possible.

After breakfast Jimmy went up to the counter and asked for the waitress. She came across nervously unsure what he wanted.

"Listen love... I am sorry about my comment. It was a joke. I was winding up my friend." He passed her a tenner,

"No hard feelings... get yourself something nice." Before she could protest, he walked away and out into the sunshine to join Ken.

As they walked along the promenade, Ken commented,

"You're in a good mood this morning. Does that mean you have work out a plan?" He looked at Jimmy trying to read his face.

"You know me too well mate. Yeah, I have a plan."

After breakfast Andy went up to the second bedroom where the desk sat with papers neatly stacked on thanks to Becky. She had sorted them and tidied. He found the details he required and came back downstairs to make a call.

The phone answered and after a few security questions to clarify it was Andy and not some con man, he was able to ask a few questions.

“I was hoping you could tell me if I have a security box linked with my account.”

“A security box Sir? I am sorry we don’t have them in our branch. You would have to transfer to a larger branch if you required one.”

“No… that’s fine. I don’t need one. I am happy to stay with you thank you.”

“Can I help you with anything else Sir?”

“No thank you.” With that they said their goodbyes and Andy replaced the receiver.

“Well, it is definitely not at the bank.”

“So where are your clues we can follow?” Becky asked.

“Don’t know.” Andy picked up the diary. “I reckon the diary has to have something in it.”

“Why?”

“Because he mentioned the diary in his will. There were jobs to finish. Maybe finding the diamond and getting it back to its rightful owner is one of the jobs.”

“Well, he has not made the job easy.”

“Very true.”

Andy opened the diary again and thumbed through until he came to around easter time. He thought this would be a good time to start. Around the beginning of May, Andy noticed a small letter F softly written in the top left-hand corner of the page.

“That’s strange…Look Becky.” She took a look and asked,

"Is there another letter or is this the only one?”

Andy turned the page and there were others, and i, n, and d.

He stated the obvious, “I spells find.”

“This must be a start to the clues.” She felt excited as she grabbed a pad and pen. She wrote the word find and then asked Andy to thumb through and see if there were more words hidden. He did so and eventually they found a message.

“Find mother and you will see; she guards the diamond until you find its home.”

“Whose mother is he on about?”

“Maybe his.”

Becky looked a bit confused,

“Does this mean we have to find her grave?”

“It’s possible. But I will have to ask my dad if he knows where she is buried.”

He went to the phone and as he picked it up, he said

“My dad is going to think I am mad.”

“Hello dad, it’s me Andy.”

“Hello son how’s it going?”

“We are fine dad… Dad this is going to sound weird… but do you know where James mum is buried?”

“Kathleen! To be honest I don’t know because your nan shut them off. I tell you what… I will try and get something from your grandad. I will let you know what I find.

”Thanks dad.”

“Why do you want to know?”

Andy had to think fast. He did not want to drag his parents into this business. Because they would worry and come over. Then possibly get dragged into it. So, he said,

“Oh, it’s one of the clauses James put in. He wants me to put flowers on her grave regularly.”

Becky looked at Andy confused. She could see he felt uncomfortable lying to his dad. After chatting a bit more, Andy put the phone down. He explained to Becky why he lied, and she agreed it was best to keep them safe and when this was over, they could come clean.

Taylor was in his office going through the report from the team that were doing a stock check of Kings Jeweller. It would be a long job, but so far it was looking as everything that should be there, was.

His phone rang, “Detective Taylor…”

“Sir this is Sergeant Rose, from Ivybridge police station. We think we have found the red allegro you are looking for.”

“Where is it?” Taylor sat up feeling a slight flutter in his stomach. He only got the feeling now and then. But when he did, he knew a new thread in his investigation was about to unravel.

“It’s parked in Ivybridge railway station sir. We were brought to its attention by railway staff as it had no parking ticket.”

“Good Sergeant… I want you to ensure no-one touches it and keep it protected until I get there.

“Yes Sir.” Rose said, but to himself as Taylor had replaced the phone abruptly.

“He’s a rude sod.”

“Who is sir?” a colleague asked.

“No-one… don’t worry.” He wasn’t going to name him as he did not know Taylor and did not know if he had friends in this station. To which could make things a bit uncomfortable for him. Rose had only been at Ivybridge for three months, he had a transfer when he moved down to Devon from London.

Back in Taylors office, Taylor was on the phone to Jerry.

"Yes, I need you right away to go to Ivybridge railway station. Daniel Kings car is there, and I am sure we will require your team. I'm sure the little sod did his sister in and scarpered on the train to god knows where." He slammed the phone down yet again before Jerry could answer.

Taylor stood up and grabbed his coat and left his office.

"Wheely… with me." He demanded and kept walking as if he would follow as commanded.

Of course, he did.

"Where are we going sir?"

"Ivybridge… I will tell you on the way… You drive." He turned slightly throwing his keys to Wheely as they walked out of the station.

In the car as they travelled Taylor brought him up to speed on the details he had so far.

"So, you think Daniel has done a runner sir."

"Yeah, and I reckon when Jerry and his team check the car over, they will find proof of Lilly's body before he dumped her."

Taylor sat in the passenger seat feeling extremely smug.

About an hour three quarters after receiving the call, Taylor and Wheely were getting out of the car at the railway station. They were met by Sergeant Rose, and he assured that no-one had touched any part of the car.

"Good… right watch and learn sergeant."

He strutted away from both sergeants towards the car.

"Is he always like this?" Rose could not contain himself.

"I'm afraid so." Wheely gave an apologetic look and they both started to move towards the car themselves.

Whispering to Wheely, Rose said

"The cheeky sod… I was on a murder squad in London before I came here."

"What made you come down?"

"The misses, she wants our children to have a more rural life. I must admit, it is beautiful…"

"Come on you two…" Taylor bellowed,

"Stop chit chatting we have work to do."

They looked in the car windows and everything looked normal. As they walked towards the back, they could smell something… unpleasant.

"Where the hell is Jerry and his team?" Taylor shouted looking towards the car park entrance. "For Christ's sake… I told him right away."

"They will be here soon Sir… Jerry and his team are pretty well organised." Wheely tried to calm Taylor, but he knew it would not work until the forensic team arrived.

Notably flies flew around the back end of the car to which Taylor was getting more irritable by the second. About ten minutes later the forensic team turned up. Jerry barely had chance to vacate his vehicle when Taylor started again.

"Where the hell have you been? We've been waiting here for bloody ages."

Jerry was in no mood to take his rantings, "Look Taylor it takes a bit longer to get our team and kit together than you are putting on your ruddy coat. So don't start on me, or I will turn around and take my team back. Then you can wait for another team. So, what will it be?" He stood glaring at Taylor.

“Okay… Okay you’re here now. I will let you get on with your job. Can you get the back done first; I think we need to see what’s in the boot? It doesn’t smell too good.” Taylor tried to sound calm and almost friendly. Almost… but it did not work.

The team dusted the back especially the catch of the boot and once they were happy with what they had, they got equipment to open the boot trying not to disturb too much.

“Oh… bugger…” Taylor stood at a distance looking into the boot with his hand over his mouth trying not to inhale. Strewn in the trunk a man in a suit… A dead… decomposed man. Daniel King

TWENTY-FIVE

Around Lunchtime, Jimmy called Davey.

“Hello Davey, my man… how’s that lovely girl of yours… Lisa?”

Davey answered cautiously, thinking crap what he wanted now. But he had to answer with a cheery voice not to show Jimmy how he felt.

“Hello Jimmy… yeah she is fine thanks.” As he spoke, he crossed his fingers.

“We are coming over. You have a van don’t you!”

Davey thought how the hell did he know. Then he remembered that when they came across the other day, Jimmy had had a good nosey about.

“Uh… yeah I do.”

“Good… I need you to drive it somewhere for me.” Davey was about to answer him, when Jimmy added, “I will tell you more when we get there.”

Jimmy got off the phone and he turned to Ken.

“Come on mate. We are meeting Davey at his lock up.”

“Right!... are you going to tell me what the plan is?” he jumped in the passenger seat, and they took off for Blandford.

“I’ll tell you when we get there.” Ken did not like being kept in the dark, but he knew not to argue. They pulled up to Davey’s lock up and got out. Jimmy locked the car and went straight into the building. Davey had sat in the small room for quite some time waiting for their arrival, nervously he stood up to greet them, putting on a brave face.

"Jimmy… good to see you again. So, what's this you want me to do?" he asked, not really wanting to know the answer.

He grabbed a seat and Ken sat also as he started to explain. After Jimmy informed both men of his plan he stated.

"This had better work."

"Jesus Jimmy… are you sure?"

"Yes I am." He stood up,

"Come on."

The three men piled into the van and Davey drove towards Dorchester. When they got to the roundabout that would take you onto the Puddletown bypass, they went straight across heading for Puddletown. At the bottom of the hill on the right they pulled into The Blue Vinney pub car park. Jimmy got out and Ken moved from the front into the back of the van.

"Christ Davey it's going to be cramped in here."

"Oh, stop moaning Ken, it won't be long." Jimmy assured.

Davey pulled away and drove back up the hill, straight over the roundabout again and onto the next one. He turned left signposted Piddlehinton. Minutes later he pulled up to the gate of Meadow View. He jumped out and opened the gate and drove through. He didn't bother to shut the gate behind him. He pulled up to the house and turned, then reversed so he was in a position to just drive out.

"Are you ready?" He called to Ken in the back.

"Yeah." Ken did not like this idea of Jimmy's at all.

Davey got out and knocked the front door of the house. This is where the plan would either go well or go tits up. He crossed his fingers behind his back.

Moments later the door opened, and Becky stood in the doorway.

"Sorry to come uninvited miss." Davey spoke humbly.

"Yes... what can I do for you?" she smiled.

Davey wanted to turn and run, she looked so beautiful and innocent. But he could not because of protecting his partner Lisa from Jimmy.

"Um... I do a lot of handy work around the area and wondered if you needed anything done. I'm a hard worker."

"I don't think so, thank you." She was about to close the door, when Davey added quickly,

"Miss, I do all sorts and I see you have a large garden. If I can't help you with it, maybe you would like to buy some tools."

He did his best to look a bit desperate. She hesitated a while then said.

"To be honest, my partner has all the tools he needs." She stopped a second, then added joking,

"Well apart from a ride on mower." She laughed and was about to shut the door. Davey was frantic not to fail, so he CALLED,

"I have one." He stood hoping this would work. She stopped and turned to him, looking at Davey strangely.

"I couldn't afford it thanks anyway."

"It's in my van... you could have a look and if you think it's too old then fine. I just need to sale something as work has been slow recently."

Was it working or not? He stood waiting.

"I ought to ask Andy about it first."

"It could be a surprise for him… I tell you what come and have a peek at it and if you thought he would like it, pop back in and get him."

Becky was not sure and if Andy had not been in the bathroom, she would have called him out. The thought of maybe getting a ride on mower for him made her smile.

"Okay… I will have a quick look." She came out and followed Davey to the back of the van. As he got to the van, he caught hold of the door handle saying,

"Are you ready?" The signal for Ken to have his balaclava on.

Becky thought it strange but stepped forwards as he opened the door. Within seconds Ken had her pulled into the back of the van and his hand placed over her mouth to stop her calling out. Davey had the door closed and he drove out as normally as possible just in case anyone saw him. As soon as they were back on the road, he picked up speed. It did not take Ken many moments to tie Becky up and gag her. He grabbed his phone out of his pocket and called Jimmy.

“How did it go Ken?”

“Like clockwork.”

“Which one do you have?”

“The female.”

“Good.” With that he stopped the call and walked up to the side door of the pub and entered a small snug. A barman came over, “What can I get you?”

“Nothing at the moment, I’m waiting for my wife. I don’t suppose you have a phone I could use do you. Mine’s gone flat.” He lied.

“Sure mate. Over in the corner.” He pointed to Jimmy’s left.

“Thanks friend.”

Jimmy walked away and waited a moment, until he was sure no-one could see or hear him. He dialled and minutes later a male voice answered.

“Hello…” he sounded a bit worried as when he came downstairs to answer the phone, he wondered why Becky had not picked it up.

"Andy..."

The deep menacing voice again. As soon as Andy heard it, he went cold and suddenly his heart was pounding, where's Becky?"

"Yes..." he answered quietly and shakily.

"Your young lady has gone for a ride; she is visiting your new best friends."

Andy fell in a heap,

"No... don't hurt her... please." He knew he sounded desperate, but he didn't care.

"We won't, as long as you do as I say."

"What? Anything... just say."

"Calm down lad... Now first thing is no police."

"I won't tell them... but they may know already."

"What do you mean?" Jimmy's blood started to boil. In his head he said to himself, keep calm.

"Well, the police came back... because of the break in and insisted they would watch our place for a few days."

“Then you had better hope they were having a tea break when we came.” He slammed the phone down and walked out the pub, just as Davey pulled in. Jimmy quickly jumped in, and they were off again heading for Blandford. At the top of the first hill there was a pull in where Davey pulled over to let Ken out of the back. Jimmy put his balaclava on and opened the doors, he stood looking at Becky.

“She’s a beauty isn’t she mate.”

“Yeah, she is, but she’s also a feisty cat. She caught me one under the chin.” Ken grinned under his balaclava. While Becky sat ridged with fear staring at two large men with blacked out faces. They shut the doors and got back in the front of the van. Neither spoke as they travelled. It was something Jimmy had insisted on.

Alan Thomas had just put the phone down after Taylor informed him of Danny’s demise, when it rang again.

“Did you forget something?” he asked, thinking it was Taylor again.

“Sorry sir!! Detective Thomas…” the voice on the phone sounded anxious.

“Yes. Thomas here what is it?”

"PC Keen here sir."

"Yes Keen... aren't you on surveillance at Meadow View?"

"Yes sir... there's been an incident sir."

"What sort of incident?"

"The young woman has been taken." He waited for an eruption of profanities, but instead Thomas asked,

"Tell me briefly what happened."

Keen attempted to inform him but was in such a state that Thomas said.

"Stay put and I will be there shortly."

Fifteen minutes later, Thomas and Collins were parked in the lay by near the manor entrance. PC Keen was stood waiting for a grilling.

"Right tell me as much detail as possible, take your time Keen."

"I was just taking over from PC Mayer when he informed me a van had just arrived at Meadow View, he thought it was a delivery van. I asked if he had seen the driver and he said yes. It was a small man wearing a cap. I said should we check it out and he said that the driver was on his own so nothing to worry about sir. PC Keen stopped for a moment, then continued, "Well, sir I took over the shift and a short while I saw the van pull away. I saw the driver and yes, he was alone. As he passed the lay by, I noticed he suddenly picked up speed. A short while later I noticed the large gate was open, so. I thought I would go and close it. While I was there, I heard a cry for help. It was Andy he was stood in the doorway of the house looking absolutely shattered. Then that's when I found out Becky had been taken sir. Then I rang you straight away sir."

"Okay Keen, I will deal with you and Mayer later. My first job is to help Andy. Stay at your post until the relief and then report to me."

"Yes Sir." Keen thought, well there goes my chance in impressing him.

Thomas and Collins pulled up to the house and before they could get out, they saw Andy rushing from the front door towards them. Collins quickly moved to him and placed an arm over his shoulder.

"Andy... let's get into the house first. I will make some tea and you and Detective Thomas can sit in the living room and have a chat."

"Have a chat! You've got to be kidding." He shouted.

"Keep calm Andy. Come on, let's do as Sergeant Collins suggested and then we can work on getting Becky back home." Thomas and Collins were used to this kind of reaction. Although they were, neither took it lightly.

When Andy cradled a mug in his hands to stop them shaking Thomas gradually and calmly talked to Andy.

"Andy... take your time. Tell me what happened."

"I don't know really... I was in the bathroom upstairs. What a bloody time to have to go, if only I wasn't there. I would have answered the ruddy door instead of Becky."

"Keep calm Andy... we all have to go at some time, and it seems that it was unfortunate you had the call of nature then... carry on."

"Well, I heard the knock on the door and Becky answered. I could not hear any exact words. When I was washing my hands, I heard the phone going. Becky would get it if I couldn't get to it. But it rang and rang. I quickly ran down the stairs to get it." Andy stopped, he sat frozen in a daze and had gone white as a sheet. Collins moved forwards and touched his arm gently.

“Andy drink, and take your time to speak.” She glanced at Hirst with concern.

“Sorry…” Andy had never felt this helpless in his life. He had to pull himself together for Becky’s sake. He cleared his throat and continued to relate the conversation on the phone.

“Right Andy…” Hirst said,

“Do you have any friends or family that could come over?”

“I don’t know who… Actually, I could call my parents. They have not seen the house yet and I know mum would love to see it. But I am worried they would be dragged into all this. Whatever this is…”

“Andy, I think it’s a good idea and Collins, can you stay here?” He turned to her.

“Yes, sir I can. The greater the number of people here the safer you will be and besides when he calls again, I will be here to listen in.”

While Andy called his parents, Thomas and Collins went out to the front and scanned the area. They didn’t think they would see anything, but it was a chance to give Andy space.

Out in the front of the house the sun shone, and it warmed their backs as they looked around. The only sounds heard were birds singing in the trees.

"I can see why anyone would love this place Gov..."

"True, it's peaceful... Ah ha... what do we have here? "he bent down and noticed a watch strewn on the gravel.

"Collins ... do you have a bag on you?"

"Yes Gov..." she passed it to him, and he carefully placed the watch in the bag. They walked back into the house as Andy replaced the receiver.

"They are coming over. I asked if they would like to come and see the house as they had not yet visited. Mum was keen. So, I suggested right now, and they agreed. I thought I would tell them what has happened when they arrive. So, mum wouldn't panic."

"Good idea... Andy is this your watch?" Thomas passed the bag to Andy so he could check.

"No!" he looked puzzled.

“Okay thanks’ Andy…I am going back to the station to check on some details. Collins will stay here with you and as soon as I can, I will be back.”

He turned and went to his car. Collins followed him out.

“I want you to keep a close eye on Andy and if he receives another call, let me know personally. I will be back as soon as possible.”

“Yes Gov…”

TWENTY-SIX

Monday 28th June, late afternoon

Thomas had had an extremely busy afternoon. On his return he sent the watch down to forensics and made a phone call to Hirst. They had brought each other up to speed on the investigation in all aspects. Hirst said he would inform Taylor and they both agreed it was imperative to find the vehicle the men travelled in as soon as possible. Thomas went to his door and called PC Mayer in.

“Yes sir.” He stood nervously in front of Thomas’s desk.

“Right… I want to know why you thought there was no need to check out this man in the van.”

“Well… Sir… we knew we were looking for two large men and the vehicle was a 4 by 4.”

“So, you in your wisdom did not think they could possibly have any help from others.” Thomas did his best not to lose his temper.

“Sorry Sir…” PC Mayer lowered his head slightly looking extremely uncomfortable.

“So, you should be. We now have a young woman in grave danger… I want a detailed description of the man driving and his van. As much as you can. Get out and start writing. And send PC Keen in.”

“Yes sir…” he left the office as quickly as possible. Moments later PC Keen entered. He like PC Mayer stood waiting for a reprimand.

“PC Keen… I realise you came to take over when the van was at Meadow View.”

“Yes sir…”

“So, you did not see it arrive!”

“No sir.”

“Okay… you said you asked PC Mayer about any visitors, and you informed me he told you of the van and driver.”

“Yes sir.” PC Keen stood rigid, his heart was pumping, and his hands were clenched tightly behind his back.

“Tell me again what happened then.”

“He said he was going to get his lunch and would be back later. Moments after he left, the van pulled out of the drive and was heading my way. I had a good look at the driver and agreed with PC Mayer that he was alone. As it went round the bend it sped up. I thought he must be late for another delivery sir.”

“Did you see anything that might help you identify the van again?”

“No sir… only that it was a dirty white. Oh, and there was a bit of cloth caught in the back door.”

“Okay PC Keen I want you to write down in as much detail you can remember of both man and van. As soon as you've done that bring it straight to me."

"Yes sir." As he left the office he exhaled in relief. Whilst the two PCs were writing their detailed reports, Thomas called the telecommunications department for information on the call.

"Detective Thomas here… I want to speak to the person working on Meadow View phone line."

"Yes sir… that would be me sir… Jackson."

"Well, Jackson do you have the details of the last call into Meadow View for me?"

"Yes sir… as soon as we received it a call was made to your office. We were told you were on your way to Meadow View."

"Have you traced the call?"

"Yes sir… it looks like it came from The Blue Vinney pub in Puddletown sir."

"Christ that's close by. Thank you, Jackson. Keep listening as I am sure he will be back in touch with Andy at Meadow View… Oh and send me the transcript please as soon as possible."

"Yes sir."

Thomas sat for a moment and thought. He noted that Keen had contacted him extremely quick due to the fact he had already left the station for Meadow View when telecommunications had tried to call. Maybe he would be someone to keep an eye on.

Thomas stood up and went to his door,

“Keen and Mayer I need those reports.”

They both stood at the same time and walked into the office with the paperwork. They stood while Thomas read through them. He noted that Keens report had a lot of detail compared with Mayer’s.

“Okay that will be all for now. Mayer, I want you back on surveillance and don’t cock up, do I make myself clear?”

“Yes sir.”

“Well, what are you waiting for?”

“Sorry sir.” He spun on his toes and left the room quickly. Meanwhile Keen stood waiting for his instructions.

“Keen I want you with me. We are going to Puddletown to the Blue Vinney. I want you to follow me in your car, as I may need to leave a car at Meadow View later.”

“Yes sir.” Keen could not work out whether he was in the clear or not over this fiasco.

They arrived at The Blue Vinney and parked at the rear. Keen stood near his car and waited for Thomas to instruct him.

“Okay Keen I want you to observe and make a note of any kind of unusual behaviour. Use your skills and take note what’s going on.”

“Yes sir.” Keen followed Thomas into the pub at the side door.

“What can I get you gents… oh sorry.” He stopped as he saw PC Keen in uniform following Thomas in.

Thomas held up his card and introduced himself to the Barman.

“Do you have a public phone?”

“Yes Detective, over there in the corner.”

“Has anyone used it today?”

“Yeah, there were a chap came in earlier. He said his phone went dead and needed the phone. He was waiting for his misses.”

“Did she turn up?”

“Don’t know, because I popped into the other bar and when I came back, he was gone.”

“Would you recognise him again?”

“Yeah, I reckon I could.”

“Good… has anyone used the phone since?”

“I don’t think so, but I can’t be sure.”

“Can you please lock off this bar area and stop anyone from using it. I need to get a team in. I am sorry. But it is extremely important we get as much information on this man. Would you be willing to come to the station, so we can get a description down as soon as possible?”

“Yeah, I can… what’s he supposed to have done?”

“I can’t tell you at the moment, but you would be helping us with a serious crime. I am sorry it’s very rude of me. What’s your name?”

“John Hunt.”

“Well John… I will inform my team you will be visiting them and ensure you get a cuppa and some biscuits while your there.” He smiled and John agreed that he would get someone to cover for him as soon as possible and get to Dorchester.

"Thank you I really appreciate your help." He shook John's hand and they left. Outside, Thomas got on his phone and arranged for the team to send someone to dust the phone in the bar and gave John's name to be expected shortly.

"Now we need to get back to Meadow View."

"Yes sir." Keen got in his car and followed Thomas out the car park and on to Meadow View.

As they neared the house, they saw PC Mayer tucked away near the entrance of the manor. He was in plain sight, but only if you knew where to look.

"Good..." Thomas murmured to his self as he drove past. When they pulled into the property, they noticed another car parked to the left by the barn. As Thomas closed his car door he was greeted by Collins.

"Gov... we have a breakthrough."

"Oh!"

"Yes Gov... Andy forgot he had the security system on constant due to the worry of unwanted visitors."

"How come he didn't say anything earlier."

"I suppose it was shock."

"Have you looked at it yet?"

"No Gov... we've only just realised. We were about to look when you turned up."

"Good timing eh..." he smiled as they followed her into the house. They walked into the living room and were introduced to Andy's parents. After all the niceties, they sat with the computer to watch the footage. Before doing so Thomas asked Andy if he wanted to let them look at it first due to the possible stress it could bring. Andy refused, he wanted to see.

"Okay... if, you are sure. If at any time you need to leave, please do so. We will understand... Okay?" Thomas waited for a response before starting the system.

"Yeah... carry on." Andy sat wondering if it was a good idea or not. As it started, Andy stood up and left the room for the kitchen, quickly followed by his mum.

"I understand his feelings." Thomas announced not to anyone in particular.

The tape started and it had a time scale, so Thomas fast forward to about half an hour before the changeover of the two PC's. For a short while all was quiet and tranquil. Then around twelve o clock, a van came in sight of the front door. All you could see at first was the colour and a blurred number plate. That was until the van reversed back towards the front door. Quickly Collins wrote down the license plate and they continued to watch. A small built young man walked right up to the front door and knocked. You could see quite a bit of his features, but not all, because he wore a baseball cap. There was a conversation, but they could not hear it. Then Becky followed the young man to the back of his van. They stopped and what looked like he said something briefly to which Becky looked a bit puzzled. He opened the doors and it all happened so fast. A large man wearing a balaclava shot forwards grabbing Becky and dragging her into the van. The doors were slammed shut by the young man and he ran to the driver's door and jumped in his seat and drove off.

"Sir..." PC Keen interrupted.

"Yes Keen..."

"Look... there's the cloth I saw, and it looks like it's part of Becky's skirt she was wearing."

"Well spotted Keen." He stopped the recording and called to Andy. He came back and just looked at them as if to say, you saw her didn't you.

"Andy that was a brilliant idea of yours to keep the security cameras on. You have helped us a great deal. I need to borrow this for a short time. I am going to ask Collins if she can stay with you all. I am going back to the station to track down the van. The stupid person driving reversed right up to your door. And gave us a perfect picture of the back of his van including the number plate."

Thomas smiled and hoped this would help Andy feel a little more at ease.

Andy just nodded and just before Thomas left... he asked Andy not to mention anything about the cctv to anyone if they received a call. He agreed and Thomas instructed Keen to stay put with the rest.

He went straight back to the station. He had called in the registration and hoped they would have some positive news on his return. He entered his office in an optimistic mood. The phone rang,

"Yes..."

"Detective Thomas... we have the name of the registered keeper."

"Great... fire away..."

"It's registered to a Davey Hawkins, from Blandford.

"Lovely job. Send me the details, Thank you."

Thomas informed the other stations with the name and address. They ran his name through the system checking who Davey Hawkins could be involved with.

Meanwhile, Taylor sat in his office annoyed at his comment to Wheely, assuming Daniel King had killed his sister and done a runner. He hated getting it wrong. How could he turn it around to make him look good? He picked up the phone and called Jerry.

"Jerry..." he tried to sound pleasant but did not quite make it. "Jerry... any information on Daniel King?"

"Well, not sure how he did it!"

"What!"

"Kill his sister, then carry her to dump her on that beach." Jerry scoffed quietly.

“Ha bloody ha. Come on man... be professional. How did he die?” Taylor was seething inside but tried to keep control.

“Okay, Taylor… Right, he has a nasty wound on his head. It looks like he’s been dead for quite some time.”

“So, we are looking for a man, a double killer.”

“It looks like it.

“Okay… let me know if you get any DNA from him other than his own.”

“Will do.”

Taylor called Wheely in…

“Wheely, sit down.” The sergeant sat cautiously, what had he done wrong now?

“Right as we know we are looking for a double killer now.”

“Yes Sir…” Wheely noticed Taylor squirm, in his chair. He had to work hard not to smile.

“We need to find his car and then we can find him. All we know is… he is in Dorset. So, we are going to Dorset.”

“We!” he looked confused.

"Yes... we. I want you to call ahead to Detective Alan Thomas and get his team to sort accommodation for us. I hope we won't be there for too long."

It was no good arguing with him. He was a stubborn old fool.

TWENTY-SEVEN

Tuesday 29th June

It was around nine in the morning. Collins was back in the office and Keen was at Meadow View with Andy and his parents. He felt privileged to be trusted with this job and was determined not to muck up.

"What time are we expecting Detective Taylor?" Thomas was busying getting everything in order to share with him.

Collins helped where she could.

"He and a Sergeant Wheely are due around eleven Gov…"

"Good that gives us time to get more answers, I hope."

He picked up his phone and called the surveillance team that were watching Davey's home.

"Any movement?"

"No Sir, not yet… oh wait a minute… he is about to get into his car. It's a tatty blue Mondeo."

"Good… keep with him and report back."

"Yes Sir."

He replaced his phone and looked up at Collins.

"You know Collins… I have a feeling we need to head for Blandford."

"Yes Gov… what about Detective Taylor?"

"Don't worry about him. He knows how to get here and besides I have a job to do. And part of it, is to follow a hunch… come on."

They grabbed their coats and left.

Travelling through Milborne St Andrew, they received a call.

“Can you get that, Peggy?” He always called her Peggy when they were alone. “Yes Gov”

“Sergeant Collins here.”

The PC on the other end spoke rapidly, “Sergeant Collins... Detective asked me to call if there were something to report.”

“Yes... fire away.”

“Well, this Davey character has been to Tesco’s stocking up. But that’s not it... he has driven to the industrial estate to a lock up and there is a car parked that is of interest to us. I think it’s the 4 by 4 we are looking for.” He sounded so excited.

Thomas had been listening and instructed the PC to keep back from the lock up and watch and wait as they were on their way.

“What’s the plan?”

“Well Peggy, I think I need to get extra help. Can you call Blandford Station?”

“Yes Gov...”

Very quickly Thomas explained his predicament and Blandford sent a couple of cars to assist.

Sat at the bottom of the hill the PC that had made the call updated Thomas with any movements.

"So, we have to approach this very carefully, we do have a young woman to protect. That's if she's there."

"Sir…"

"Yes PC…"

"We saw him take in the shopping he had bought earlier."

"And…"

"Well, we thought he would take it back home as he lives close by."

"Well observed… He could be just popping in to pick something up before going back home… No… he would have left it in the car. Ah here is our back up."

Thomas took a short time instructing the others what he wanted from them.

Around five minutes later, Collins walked towards the lock up and tapped on the side door.

"Who is it?" a slightly agitated voice came from behind the door.

"Sorry… I seem to be lost… I wonder if you can help me?" Collins hesitated a moment, then added,

"I was told there was a gym at the top of this lane."

It was from information given by the Blandford police that helped her. As there was a gym… but in the next lane across.

"You're in the wrong lane miss." Davey called back.

"Which lane do you mean?"

Collins was listening as close to the door as possible.

"Crap…" came a hushed voice, definitely different to Davey's. As soon as she heard it, she raised her arm to signal the team.

"Look missy, I am busy at the moment… just go back down the lane to the bottom and turn left, then left again, it's up there."

She stood as close as possible and called out,

"Thank you."

As she had them concentrating on her, Davey, Jimmy, and Ken never noticed others approaching the building.

Bang… Bang… Thomas thumped the door.

"Police… Davey open up." He shouted.

Jimmy and Ken glared at Davey.

"What the fuck have you done?" Jimmy exploded.

"What do we do?" Ken asked.

Jimmy quickly walked up to Becky and hissed.

"You had better play along miss, or your young man will get hurt. Do I make myself clear?"

Becky was frightened of him, so she nodded vigorously. He quickly untied her and he made Ken stand close to her.

Jimmy took off his balaclava and nodded for Ken to do also. Ken looked confused and thought bloody hell now the girl will die as she can identify us.

Seconds later. Davey opened the door slowly. Thomas stepped in, with Collins right behind. As soon as Collins caught sight of Becky, she made a face to say keep quiet. All the while hoping the others had not noticed. Becky gave a short, small nod and Collins relaxed a bit.

"Davey Hawkins… is that your blue Mondeo outside?"

"Yes… why? It's taxed and insured…" Davey sounded agitated.

Thomas turned towards Jimmy and Ken.

"So would I be right to say the Range Rover is…"

Jimmy quickly said,

"It's mine and yes it also is taxed and insured." He smiled looking right into Thomas's face.

"Thank you, gentlemen, … Can I ask you sir, what brings you here today?"

"We are doing business with Davey… isn't that right Davey?"

"Um… yes Jimmy."

If looks could kill, Davey would have dropped down dead.

"What type of business… Jimmy?" Thomas smiled knowing he had an advantage.

"Uh… uh… Crap." Jimmy made a run for the door and knocked Collins over in doing so. Ken followed, but by then Thomas was aware and stuck his foot out quickly, tripping him. He fell right into the side of the door, to which a couple of PC's caught hold of him. Jimmy thought he would escape but had a surprise waiting for him in the form of four PC's.

"I think Davey, you need to come with us."

Collins got up and brushed herself down and went right over to Becky and checked on her.

Becky stood up and flung her arms round Collins.

"You're okay now Becky. Did they hurt you?"

"No… apart from tying me up and gagging me."

On the way back, Collins drove, and Thomas called Keen.

"PC Keen."

"Yes Sir…"

"How is Andy fairing?"

"He is holding up Sir."

"Can you put him on the phone please?"

Moments later Andy spoke.

"Hello Detective, have you found Becky? Is she alright?" He spoke so fast.

"I'm fine Andy." Thomas had passed the phone to her. Andy dropped to the floor. "Becky... love are you alright?" He was almost crying, but quickly pulled himself together. Thomas took the phone back and spoke

"Andy... she is fine don't worry. Now we are taking Becky to the station to check her over and take a statement. If you can put PC Keen back on the line for me, please."

Reluctantly, he passed the phone back.

"Keen... I want you to bring Andy in. Becky will need him here."

"Yes Sir."

When they arrived at the station, Thomas noticed a couple of men at the reception desk.

"Detective Taylor and Sergeant Wheely to see Detective Alan Thomas."

The woman behind the desk smiled and turned her head slightly looking behind Taylor. He was about to repeat when... "Detective Taylor... Sergeant Wheely... you made good time." He put out his hand, "Detective Thomas, good to meet you."

Taylor looked surprised, as most did when they first met him. As he was rather a young man to be a detective.

“Follow me Taylor, I think I have someone you would like to meet.”

“We don’t have time Thomas. we need to find the car.”

“Don’t worry about that.” Thomas walked in front smiling from ear to ear.

Thomas interviewed Jimmy while Taylor watched from another room. Jimmy did his utmost to deny everything, but once Thomas presented him with the proof like fingerprints at Meadow View and Becky’s interview of events, he knew he could not escape prosecution. As Thomas stood to leave the room, he stopped and turned back to Jimmy. “Oh, Jimmy… there is someone else that would like a word with you.”

“What? I’ve already admitted breaking and entering the house and regrettably taking the girl. So, who the fuck wants to speak to me now?”

“I do...” Taylor entered the room followed by Wheely and introduced himself. He went through the procedures for the tape and sat opposite Jimmy. Wheely stood at the back listening.

"Ok Jimmy… where do we start? Do you know a Daniel King?"

"No… why should I?" Jimmy sat rigid and he started to get palpitations.

"That's funny Jimmy… because we found your DNA all over Daniels body." Taylor sat back and just stared at him.

Not a word.

So, Taylor continued,

"Do you know a Lilly King?"

"No." the answer came back very quickly. Almost too quickly.

"Funny. I thought you would say that. So, it's strange that we should find your prints in the place where Lilly was killed."

"How do you know where she was killed?"

"You don't seem to be surprised to hear she was killed."

He did not answer.

"Okay Jimmy… I think it's about time you told us what happened… Ken has told us his side so why don't you tell me yours."

"He can't have… he had nothing to do with it." Jimmy stopped abruptly.

"Shit..."

Taylor just sat and waited a moment.

"Look Jimmy... why don't you tell me what happened."

TWENTY-EIGHT

On the morning of Monday 14th June around ten thirty. The doorbell sounded as Jimmy entered Kings Jeweller. He looked around to make sure no one else was in there. King came from the back and stopped dead when he saw Jimmy turning a lock on the door. Trying to keep calm he greeted him.

"Hello sir, can I help you?"

"Are you King?" Jimmy spoke slowly and dedicated to keeping as calm as he could.

"Um yes I am Mr. King. Do I know you?"

"The name is Smith. My wife came here about two years ago."

"Right... so. How can I help you?" his mind whirled over and over. Jimmy walked over to the counter and placed the box on the glass top.

"Take a look at this."

King took it gingerly and opened the box. He did his best not to show any emotion but failed.

"That… That is beautiful." He stuttered.

"It is Mr. King, but you would know as you made it." Jimmy stood close and towered over King as he kept his eyes on him.

"Oh yes, now I remember a beautiful blue diamond. So, what can I help you with?"

"Look at it again…" he seethed.

He took it and held it close, small beads of sweat appeared on his forehead. He hoped Jimmy had not noticed. But he had.

"**Where is it?**" Jimmy shouted.

"What?" King's voice quivered.

"My blue diamond, you thief." He spat.

"Here… it's here." King held it towards Jimmy his arm trembling.

"**Liar**… tell me. What have you done with it?"

"Nothing, I don't know what you mean."

Jimmy punched him hard.

He pulled King out to the back room of his shop. He had to pay; no-one gets one over on Jimmy. He had to think fast now. He saw a sign that said closed for lunch, so he put it on the door to stop anyone attempting to enter. Back in the confines of the storage area, lay King, barely conscious. Jimmy bent down and slapped his face a couple of times.

"Wake up King… Wake up. dam it man…"

A flicker of acknowledgement as he stirred slowly.

"Good boy… now come on, King what's your first name? I can't keep calling you King if we're to be friends can I."

He looked up at Jimmy with a glimmer of hope,

"Danny… my names Danny."

"Well Danny boy, if you want to see tomorrow then you had better tell me what you've done with my diamond." He gave him another slap. Danny just lay there too petrified to move. Jimmy raised his fist for another punch when Danny caved in.

"Okay! Okay…" he attempted to take a deep breath but coughed as he swallowed some blood that had gone down his throat from the punch that had knocked him out.

"I'm waiting!" Jimmy still held his fist high.

"I... I hid it." He started to shake uncontrollably.

"Where?"

"In a book on my shelves upstairs. But do not go up, my sister Lily's up there. You will frighten her. I will get it for you."

"What's the name of the book?"

"Stolen." Danny attempted to get up, but Jimmy was not having any of it. Fury had raised its ugly head again. The cheek of it all, Stolen, he was taking the mick. Jimmy punched him hard in the face and Danny's head went back and he cracked his skull on the edge of a solid wooden shelf.

"Crap..." Jimmy hissed, and he stood up.

The dead body of King lay in a crumpled heap. Jimmy turned away and saw the narrow stairs winding up to the flat above. Slowly he climbed them and opened the door at the top.

He heard a female voice from a back room.

"What time is it, Danny? Not lunch time yet!"

"No, it's not." Jimmy replied calmly.

"Who the hell are you?" Lily came into the room. She stood about five feet two and carried a lot more weight than she should. Her short curly hair was damp as she had just had a shower.

"I'm your new friend," he sneered.

"Where's Danny?" she stood frozen to the spot.

"He's sleeping downstairs."

She looked confused,

"what do you mean? He wouldn't sleep there."

"He is now… permanently."

She almost fell in a heap on the floor.

"Christ! What happened?" she tried to keep calm as she spoke. knowing, by the look of Jimmy that he may be responsible.

"Your Danny was nothing but a thieving little bastard. "

"What! He wouldn't steal anything."

"No...?" Jimmy scanned the room and saw a bookcase with some books stacked on most shelves.

"What do you want? The jewellery is downstairs. There's nothing up here."

"Are you sure?" he walked over to the bookcase and starting to run his finger across the books. After checking each one again he turned onto her again.

"Where is it?"

"What?"

"The book."

"What book?"

"Stolen."

"That's all the books we have." She looked unsure as to what would happen next.

Jimmy went mad, he started to ransack the place checking every cupboard and every hiding place he could think of.

In frustration he turned on Lily and grabbed her arm. He sat her down on the settee and bent close and spoke in her ear.

"Where is the book?" he hissed.

"I... I don't know." She screwed up her eyes expecting to be hit.

"Don't lie to me Lily, I don't like liars. You know what happens to liars don't you."

She opened her eyes slowly and saw his angry face close to hers. She started to cry uncontrollably. As she cried, she blurted,

"I took some of Danny's books to the local book sale. It might have been amongst them."

She looked terrified.

"Hell… did you sell them? Or did you give them to someone else to sell."

"I… I sold them… "very quickly she added,

"I sold them to a man I always see at the book sale. He bought them all, the whole box."

"Do you know his name?" Jimmy felt desperate and his heart was thumping in his chest.

"No… but I know he stays at Jake's sometimes."

"Whose Jake and where does he live?" the questions were coming out fast and furious.

"Um… "she hesitated a moment not wanting to put him in danger. But if she did not tell him. She would be. As Lily spoke, she thought as soon as he goes, I will call Jake to warn him.

"He is a friend from way back. He lives on the coastline near Looe."

Jimmy stood up and looked for a piece of paper and pen. He found them on a side table, and he threw them at Lily.

"Write down his address." She fumbled picking up the pen and he shouted, "Quickly, I haven't all day."

She wrote as quickly as possible; her hands shook, and you could see this in the writing. Passing it to Jimmy, she cried

"You've got what you want, now leave me alone."

He checked the address and shoved it in his pocket. Turning to her he said,

"I'm sorry, but you know too much and can identify me."

"NO!" she cried.

Jimmy stood for a while, not sure what to do. When he woke this morning, he never thought he would be responsible for the death of two people. He ran down the stairs and went to the back door of the shop. He opened the door carefully and sighed when he realised it opened to a small back yard and parked in the yard was a small car. Danny's car. Jimmy quickly hunted for the keys and found them. They were hung up close to the back door. It took him quite a while to get the couple into the car and clean every surface he could think of.

He drove Danny's car out to Trebarwith and when he was sure no one else was around, he dumped Lilly on the pebbled beach. He then travelled to Ivybridge train station. He left the car with Danny in the boot.

It took him around three hours by the time he had to wait to get rid of Lily. Parking in Ivybridge Railway station car park. Then catching a train to Par. Taking two & half hours back, then a half hour journey to Fowey to pick up his car.

Jimmy asked Taylor where they found his prints in the flat.

"On a pen."

"Fuck… I forgot I got the old woman to write the address down for me."

"Why did you leave Danny at the train station?" Taylor interrupted.

"Because if you lot found his car, I thought some idiot in the police force would think he did a runner after killing his sister."

"Look... it was an accident, Danny fell and hit his head." Jimmy started to realise the amount of trouble he was in.

"Maybe... but killing his sister, then dumping both bodies..." Taylor made a grim face.

"Interview finished at one-thirty pm, Detective Taylor leaving the room. Wheely you can read him his rights and finish up".

TWENTY-NINE

Becky had a thorough check at the police station and apart from dehydration and a few grazes, she was good to go home. Andy hugged her as if he couldn't or would not let her go.

"I'm alright Andy, let's go home." She kissed him and they both followed Keen out to the car. Keen drove them home and as the couple got out of the car, they were greeted by Andy's parents with lots of hugs and kisses.

They all sat around the kitchen table drinking coffee. Becky announced she wanted to put it all behind her.

“We will… but Becky… we still haven’t found the diamond.” Andy stated softly hoping he would not upset her.

“I know. So, let’s concentrate on finding it… and get it back to its rightful owner.” She smiled at Andy to reassure him; she was made of stronger stuff.

John… Andy’s dad announced,

“I went to see your granddad a few days ago and he brought out some old photos.” He looked at Anne his wife.

“Anne, love do you have them?”

“Yes… Just a minute.” She stood up and went to her bag and pulled out a couple of old photographs, placing them on the table in front of Andy. John reached out and tapped one,

“This is the wedding photo of James parents Kathleen and William.” He hesitated while Andy and Becky scanned the picture.

“Who’s that behind them?” he pointed towards an adult bridesmaid.

"I'm afraid that is Alice... the young woman that had a baby by William."

Andy asked,

"Do we know her surname?"

"No... I'm afraid not... but there is some writing on the back of the photo." He picked it up and turned it over and placed it back on the table. Andy read it out,

"William & Kathleen and 'The Floozie Alice'.

"Oh!" Becky just stared at it for a moment, then picked up another picture. This was of lots of people enjoying themselves in what looked like a village hall.

"Is this the reception?

"Yes Becky, We are not sure why Andy's great gran kept this one."

"What do you mean?"

It was Anne that answered,

"Well, dear... If you look carefully, in the picture is little Molly, Alice's daughter. But maybe it was kept because your great granddad is in it, and he looks really handsome."

"I can see where Andy gets his looks." She laughed.

Andy felt good seeing Becky happy. He knew she could have moments of anxiety; they had been informed by the medical examiner at the station. But he would be there for her and help her through.

"I wonder where she is now?" Andy surmised.

"Do you think James knew he had a half-sister?" Becky asked while she held the photo looking at it.

"If he did… well, surely he would have left the house to her."

His dad disagreed,

"No lad… he stated it had to be a male. So, something made him go off women."

"I can't see that, John." Mary interrupted and then continued,

"It was his father that did wrong, not his mother."

"True…"

Andy's parents stayed for another day and then they had to go home. Anne had her sister coming over to stay. They promised to visit again as soon as possible.

Andy and Becky waved them goodbye and went back in the house. They entered the living room and slumped down on the settee together.

"It's good to have the place to ourselves again." Andy stated. Becky looked at him in a curious way. He noticed and added,

"Oh, it was good to see them, and they helped a lot... but it's exhausting having to entertain. I just love it being you and me." They kissed and sat for a while in silence. Andy broke the silence saying,

"We now have photos of Molly... I wonder if James had any when his parents died. I mean he would have had some of their things. It wouldn't have all gone to my great nana."

"True... so where could we look?"

There were a couple of pictures in the snug. They both got up and went into the small room. The photos were in a pile on the piano. Becky picked them up and the couple looked at them. They were no good. There was a picture of a small boy and girl playing together and when she turned it over it read, 'William and Matilda'.

"So, that's your great grandma."

"They looked happy there, it's a shame they fell out."

"I know."

The next place they looked was up in the second bedroom. On the small desk where still piles of paperwork stacked. So, carefully they sorted through them. Near the bottom of one pile Andy came across another photo of a small girl smiling. He turned it over in hope of finding some writing on the back. He was not disappointed. 'Molly aged six, if you want to see her here is our number... 0181 555 231'.

"That's an old London number, the code has changed to 020." Andy said.

"I wonder why James kept it?"

"I'm not sure... but... shall I try the number?"

"Don't be daft, that is years ago, she wouldn't still live there wherever there is." Becky laughed.

"Well, there's only one way to find out." He held the photo and went down to the living room to the phone. Becky followed interested,

"What are you going to say?"

"Um... I could ask first if it is Molly, That's if a female answers the phone."

"If not... then what?"

"I'll wing it." He smiled.

He rang the number with the new dialling code and waited. It did ring. He sat with palpitations thumping away in his chest. Just as he was about to put the phone down, he heard a frail voice answer.

"555 231... "

Andy froze a moment wondering if he should put the phone down but changed his mind as the elderly female voice on the other end may think she had received a crank call and he did not want to frighten her.

"Um... Hello... I am trying to reach Molly..."

There was silence for a moment, then the woman said,

"This is Molly... have you found it?"

"Sorry... found what?"

"Oh, sorry dear, I thought you were calling in answer to my advert. Who is this?" she sounded guarded.

"I'm sorry, let me introduce myself. My name is Andy. If you are the Molly, I am looking for... then I am related to your dad several times removed."

"I never knew my dad. Only his name."

"Would his name have been William Keely?"

She gasped and a slight cry.

"Oh, please forgive me, I didn't want to upset you. I shouldn't have called." Andy was about to put the phone down when, Molly asked, "How did you find my number if you didn't see my advert?"

"It's a long story..." Andy did his best to keep it short and tried to explain what had happened.

"I see... well it's a good job I've lived here all my life."

"Very true... Um Molly... you said you place an advert because you lost something!"

"Yes dear, but I'm afraid I didn't lose it. It was stolen."

"Oh, I'm sorry to hear that. Can't the police do anything?"

“No dear they reckon it was a young lad that took it not knowing it’s worth. So, he’s probably thrown it away.”

“Do you mind if I ask you what was stolen?”

“It’s an extremely rare blue diamond. It is the only thing I had from my father. You see his father acquired the opportunity to obtain some diamonds.

With the discovery of diamonds in 1867 it dramatically altered the economic and political structure of southern Africa. Creating greater divisions between British and Boer, white and black, rich, and poor. At the turn of the century south Africa had an extremely valuable resource that attracted foreign capital and large-scale immigration. So, more foreign capital had been invested in south Africa. The white population grew, and hundreds and thousands of Africans sought work each year as the mine developed. But not all the newfound wealth was shared equally you know.”

Andy went as white as a sheet and Becky went frantic wondering. He took a deep breath,

“Molly… I think your diamond is in Dorset somewhere.”

“What… why would you think that?”

He tried to explain without any of the gory details.

“I and my partner Becky are trying to find it. But James your half-brother hid it well. Molly would it be okay if we call again? We will continue to look and if we are lucky, I can return it to you.”

She gave a little cry and apologised,

”Sorry young man… it’s just that it’s been over two years and not a day has gone by, I haven’t hoped for this call.”

“Can I ask a delicate question?” Andy was not sure if he should.

“Yes dear.”

“Did your father contact you?”

“No dear… my mother said he had another life with a wife and children. But she told me he loved me that’s why he gave her his most precious item he had to help her financially.”

“So, the diamond was Williams.”

“Yes dear. It was. I grew up thinking he gave it to her to help me. But during my mother’s last days, she told me she had to blackmail him into giving it to her for me, to stop my mother telling her friend Kathleen about their affair."

"Oh dear." Andy did not know what to say.

"No worries, because I grew up thinking good about my father and he had no choice, he had another family to support."

"How come your mother did not cash it in for money?"

"She said it was mine and if I wanted, I could. But it was the only thing I had of his, so, I kept it."

Andy and Molly exchange phone numbers and he promised to call her soon to keep her up to date.

When he replaced the phone Becky just sat there and spoke

"Wow... I can't believe it."

He relayed everything to her, and they sat shell shocked together.

"I cannot believe that we know who owns this diamond."

"I know Becky... but we've still got to find it."

THIRTY

Thursday 1st July

Becky and Andy woke around eight and just laid in each other's arms only glad to be together. The sun shone through the window like a ray of hope. After they had showered and dressed, Becky suggested they take another long look around the house again. They had another good reason to find the diamond now.

Becky sat on the bed brushing her hair, her mind wandered. She just surveyed the room and the picture that always sat by the bed caught her eye.

"We must get some new glass for this picture Andy."

"Yeah, I suppose so. Do we know who it is?"

"No… but maybe…"

“What are you doing?” he asked as she started to try and take the frame apart.

“Well, we need to get the glass out to get the size needed to replace it. And I wondered if a name of this beautiful woman is written on the back, as so many of James photos have something on the back.”

“That’s a brilliant idea.” Andy came across and sat next to her. She struggled getting the back off the chunky frame. As the last clip released the covering, she carefully turned it over and lifted it away.

“Oh my God…”

Down in the living room Andy picked up the phone and dialled.

“555 231… “

“Molly it’s Andy and Becky from Dorset.”

“Oh, hello dear, we only talked yesterday, do you have some news for me?”

“Yes, Molly we do… we found your diamond.”

Molly was in tears, and it took a while for Andy to explain where it was hidden.

After some time chatting, they arranged a meeting. Molly insisted she wanted to come down and meet Andy and Becky and she wished to see where her half-brother lived. So, Molly said an awfully close friend of hers would bring her down and they planned to meet the following day around midday at Meadow View.

Molly brought proof of ownership of her diamond with her, and Andy had asked for Alan Thomas to be present so he could witness the return and be able to close the case.

Becky worked all morning making a lovely buffet lunch for them all.

Dead on twelve o'clock. A large old car pulled into Meadow View and Alan Thomas and Andy greeted Molly and her friend James. She certainly looked well off, her refined clothes and jewellery that shone in the sunshine gave her an air of royalty. After all the niceties they all sat in the living room and once settled, Becky went to a small drawer where she took out the beautiful blue diamond. Carefully she placed it in Molly's hand. Molly wept again but with joy. Becky found it hard to see the diamond go as it was so beautiful, but she knew it would be more wonderful to give it back to Molly.

"Tell me again how you found it please." Molly asked as she looked at her diamond.

Becky explained and she also showed Molly the picture. The picture was of Kathleen, James Mother. On the back written... 'keep it safe mum'

Molly sat smiling and then said,

"You know it's ironic... putting it with Kathleen."

"What do you mean?" Andy asked.

"It should have been hers; the diamond should have been hers."

Detective Thomas stood up and announced he should leave as it was a family affair and he had proof it belonged to Molly. He asked for her to put it in writing for their records so he could close up the case. She agreed and Andy and Becky shook his hand thanking him for all he had done for them.

"Are you sure you won't stay for food?"

"No thank you."

After he had gone, they all sat down to some lunch and talked constantly. When they finished their food, they went back into the living room. Molly wanted Andy and Becky to sit with her.

They sat opposite and waited for her to speak.

“Andy… Becky… I have had a long chat with James my close and very dear friend on the way down. And… I have decided that I want you to have my diamond.”

“No… no… we can’t take it. It’s yours from your father.” Andy was adamant.

“Andy dear… I have been without it for two years and I have realised that my time is nearly up. I want to be sure that it has a loving home. I have visited your home and I feel an inner peace and I realise my diamond belongs here; besides I have no family, apart from you”. She smiled.

“But…”

“No… James will tell you… when I make up my mind then it’s no use arguing. Still, I don’t need it financially as you can see, I am lucky to be well off.” She smiled and passed the diamond to Andy.

“I… I don’t know what to say.”

“Say you will make Becky an honest woman, I know a good one when I see one. Just be happy here.” She stood up to leave and as she went for the door, she turned,

“Oh, by the way, I named the diamond ‘The Keely diamond.”

“After your father?” Andy asked.

“Yes and no… Yes because of his name but also, I found out that Keely means beautiful.”

There is a song in the walls of this house
that raises my spirits in quiet moments,
when the wind becomes still air, and it
sounds as if the world has paused to take a
moment to breathe, I know we will be happy
here. Now Becky has agreed to be my wife,
I have found my inner peace and realise
that I am home...

Printed in Great Britain
by Amazon

64590498R00220